W9-ABE-565

AUNT MARIA

ALSO BY

Diana Wynne Jones

Archer's Goon

Believing is Seeing: *Seven Stories*

Castle in the Air

Dark Lord of Derkholm

Dogsbody

Eight Days of Luke

Fire and Hemlock

Hexwood

Hidden Turnings:
A Collection of Stories Through Time and Space

The Homeward Bounders

Howl's Moving Castle

The Merlin Conspiracy

The Ogre Downstairs

Power of Three

Stopping for a Spell

A Tale of Time City

The Time of the Ghost

Warlock at the Wheel and Other Stories

Wild Robert

Witch's Business
Year of the Griffin
Yes, Dear

THE WORLDS OF CHRESTOMANCI
Book 1: Charmed Life
Book 2: The Lives of Christopher Chant
Book 3: The Magicians of Caprona
Book 4: Witch Week
Mixed Magics: *Four Tales of Chrestomanci*
The Chronicles of Chrestomanci, Volume 1
(Contains books 1 and 2)
The Chronicles of Chrestomanci, Volume 2
(Contains books 3 and 4)

THE DALEMARK QUARTET
Book 1: Cart and Cwidder
Book 2: Drowned Ammet
Book 3: The Spellcoats
Book 4: The Crown of Dalemark

Diana Wynne Jones

GREENWILLOW BOOKS
An Imprint of HarperCollins*Publishers*

Aunt Maria

First published in Great Britain in 1991 by Methuen Children's Books Ltd.
First published in the United States in 1991 by Greenwillow Books.
Reissued in 2003 by Greenwillow Books, an imprint of HarperCollins Publishers.

 Printed in the United States of America. For information address HarperCollins Children's Books, a division of HarperCollins Publishers, 1350 Avenue of the Americas, New York, NY 10019. www.harperchildrens.com

The text of this book is set in Cochin.

Library of Congress Cataloging-in-Publication Data

Jones, Diana Wynne.
Aunt Maria / by Diana Wynne Jones.
p. cm.
Summary: While visiting and caring for Great-aunt Maria,
Mig and Chris discover that their "helpless" relative has frightening powers.
ISBN 0-688-10611-0
[1. Great-aunts—Fiction. 2. Magic—Fiction.] I. Title.
PZ7.J684Bl 1992 [Fic]—dc20 90-24742 CIP AC

New Greenwillow Edition, 2003: ISBN 0-06-623742-4
10 9 8 7 6 5 4 3 2 1

This book
is for Elly

AUNT MARIA

oNe

We have had Aunt Maria ever since Dad died. If that sounds as if we have the plague, that is what I mean. You have to call this plague *Ma-rye-ah.* Aunt Maria insists you say her name like that. Chris says it is more like that card game, where the one who wins the queen of spades loses the game. "Black Maria," it is called. Maybe he is right.

That is the first thing I wrote in the locked journal Dad gave me that awful Christmas, but I think it needs more explanation, so I will squeeze some in. Dad left early in December and took the car. He rang up suddenly from France, saying he had gone away with a lady called Verena Bland and wouldn't be coming back.

"Verena Bland!" Mum said. "What an awful name!" But she said it in a way which meant that wasn't the only awful thing. Chris doesn't get on with Dad. He said, "Good riddance!" and then got very annoyed with me because all I seemed to be able to think of was that Dad had gone off with the story I was writing hidden in our car in the space on top of the radio. I mean, I *was* upset about Dad, but that was the way it took me. At that time I thought the story was going to be a masterpiece and I wanted it back.

Of course Dad had to come back. That was rather typical. He had left a whole lot of stuff he needed. He came and fetched it at Christmas. I think Verena Bland had disappeared by then, because he came with a necklace for Mum and a new calculator for Chris. And he gave me this lovely fat notebook that locks with a little key. I was so pleased about it that I forgot to ask for my story from the car, and then I forgot it completely because Mum and Dad had a whole series of hard, snarling rows, and Mum ended up saying she wanted a divorce. I still can't get over it being *Mum* who did! Nor could Dad, I think. He got very angry and stormed out of the house and into our car and drove away without all the stuff he had come to fetch. But my story went with him.

He must have driven off to see Aunt Maria in Cranbury-on-Sea. He was always very dutiful about Aunt Maria, even though she is only his aunt by marriage. But he never got there, because the car skidded on some ice going over Cranbury Head and went over the cliff into the sea. The tide was up, so he could have been all right, even so. But there was something wrong with the door on the driver's side. It had been like that for six months and you had to crawl in through the other door. The police think the passenger door burst open and the sea came in and swept him away while he was stunned. The seat belt was undone, but he may have forgotten to fasten it. He often did forget. Anyway, they still haven't found him.

Inquest adjourned. That is the next thing I wrote. Mum doesn't know if she's a widow or a divorcée or a married lady. Chris says, "Widow." He feels bad about saying, "Good riddance!" the way he did before, and he got very annoyed with me when I said Dad could have been picked up by a submarine that didn't speak English or swum to France or something. "There goes Mig with her happy endings again," Chris said. But I don't care. I *like* happy endings. And I asked Chris why something should be truer just because it's unhappy. He couldn't answer.

Mum has gone all guilty and agonizing. She sent Neil Holstrom packing, and I thought Neil was going to be her boyfriend. Actually, even when I wrote that I wasn't sure Mum liked Neil Holstrom, but I wanted to be fair. Neil reminded me of an earwig. All Mum did was buy Neil's nasty little car off him, which was hard on Neil, even though I was glad to see the back of him. But it was true about Mum going all guilty. Chris and I went rather strange, too—sort of nervous and soggy at the same time—and couldn't settle down to do anything. There are huge gaps in the notebook when I couldn't be bothered to write things in it.

Mum's worst guilt was about Aunt Maria. She said it was her fault Dad had gone driving off on icy roads to see Aunt Maria. Aunt Maria took to making the lady who lived with her ring up twice a day to make sure we were all right. Mum said Aunt Maria had had quite as much of a shock as we had, and we were to be nice to her. So we were all far too nice to Aunt Maria. And suddenly we had gone too far to start being nasty. Aunt Maria kept ringing up. If we weren't in, or if it was only Chris at home and he didn't answer the phone, Aunt Maria telephoned all our friends, even Neil Holstrom, and anyone else she could get hold of, and told them that *we*'d disappeared now and she was ill with worry. She rang our doctor and our dentist and found out how to ring Mum's boss when he was at home. It got so embarrassing that we had to make sure one of us was always in the house from four o'clock onward to answer the phone.

It was usually me who answered. Mum worked late a lot around then, so that she could get off work and spend Easter with us. The next thing in my notebook is about Aunt Maria phoning.

Chris has a real instinct for when it's going to be Aunt Maria. He says the phone rings in a special, gently persistent way, with a clang of steel under the gentleness. He gathers up his books the moment it starts and makes for the door, shouting, "You answer it, Mig. I'm working."

Even if Chris isn't there to warn me, I know it's going to be Aunt Maria because the first person I hear is the operator, sounding annoyed and harassed. Aunt Maria always grandly forgets that you can look up numbers and then dial them. She makes Lavinia, the lady who looks after her, go through the operator every time. Lavinia never speaks. You just hear Aunt Maria's voice distantly shouting, "Have you got through, Lavinia?" and then a clatter as Aunt Maria seizes the phone. "Is that you, Naomi, dear?" she says urgently. "Where's Chris?"

I never learn. I always hold the phone too near my ear. She knows London is a long way away from Cranbury, so she shouts. And you have to shout back or she yells that you are muttering. "This is Mig, Auntie," I shout back. "I prefer to be called Mig." I say that every time, but Aunt Maria never will call me anything but Naomi, because I was called Naomi Margaret after her daughter who died. Then I transfer the receiver to my other ear and rub the first one. I know that she's shouting to know where Chris is again. "Chris is working!" I shriek. "Math!"

She respects that. Chris has somehow managed to fix it in her mind that he is a Mathematical Genius and His

Work Is Sacred. I wish I knew how he did. I would like to fix it in her mind that I am going to be a Great Writer and My Time Is Precious, but she seems to think only boys have the right to have ambitions.

Aunt Maria's voice takes on a boomingly reproachful note. "I'm very worried about Chris," she says, as if that is my fault. "I don't think he gets enough fresh air."

That starts the tricky bit. I have to convince her that Chris gets plenty of fresh air without telling her how he gets it. If I say he goes to see his friends, then either she says Chris is neglecting his work or she rings his friends to check. I nearly died the time she rang Andy. I want Andy to think well of me. But if I leave it too vague, Aunt Maria becomes convinced that Chris is in Bad Company. She will ring Chris's form master then. I nearly died when she did that, too. Mr. Norris asked me about Aunt Maria every time he passed me in the corridor. She obviously scarred his soul.

But I've learned how to do it now. Chris will be surprised to know that he plays tennis every day with a friend who doesn't have a phone. Then I have to do the same for Mum. Mum plays tennis, too, with the phoneless friend's Mum—who is a widow, in case Aunt Maria gets worried about that. Then we get on to me. For some reason, I am not supposed to do anything, even get fresh air. Aunt Maria says, "And what a good little girl you are, Naomi, working away, keeping house for your mother!"

I agree with this, for the sake of peace, though it always makes me want to say, "Well, really I'm just off to burn the church down on my way to the nudist colony."

After that she goes on to her latest theories about what really happened to Dad, and then to how upset she is. All I can do there is shout a soothing "Ye—es!" every so often. That part makes me feel awful. But I have to keep listening, because that part always leads to us being the only family she's got now, and then, "So when are you all coming to Cranbury to visit me?"

This is where I get truly artful. Aunt Maria gets enticing. She says, "Chris can have the sofa, and if Lavinia moves down to the little room, you and Betty can share Lavinia's room."

"How *kind*!" I say. "But I'm afraid Chris has this exam." You wouldn't believe how often Chris has exams. Chris doesn't mind. He gives me suggestions. One thing Chris and I were really determined on was that we were not, *ever*, going to visit Aunt Maria in Cranbury-on-Sea. We both have dreadful memories of going there as small children.

Now of course we had other reasons. Would you want to go and stay in the place your father didn't quite get to before he died? No. So I put Aunt Maria off. I did it beautifully. I kept it all politely vague for months, and we were looking forward to the Easter holidays, when Mum answered the phone one evening I was out and undid all my good work in seconds. I got back to find she had agreed for us to spend Easter with Aunt Maria.

Chris and I were furious. I said I thought it was very unfeeling of Aunt Maria to make us go. Chris said, "There's no reason to have anything to do with her, Mum. She was only Dad's aunt by marriage. She's got no claim."

But Mum's guilt was working overtime. She said, "It would be horrible not to go if she wants us. She's a poor lonely old lady. Dad meant a lot to her. It will make her terribly happy to have us there. We're going. It would be really selfish not to."

So here we all are at Aunt Maria's house in Cranbury-on-Sea. We only got here this evening and I'm so depressed already that I decided to write it all down. Mum said that if I *am* going to write rude things about Aunt Maria, I'll have to make sure she can't read it. So I sighed heavily and decided to use my hardback notebook with the lock on it. I was going to use most of it for my chart of King Arthur's Knights and pop groups, because I didn't want Chris to find those and jeer, but I'd rather have Chris on to me than Aunt Maria any day. This will be under lock and key when I've written it down.

Unfortunately, Mum drove us down in Neil's car. It's small and slow, with so little space for people that Chris's guitar was digging into me all the way; and there are horrible crunching noises from the suspension when you drive with luggage in. Chris and I wanted to go by train. That way we wouldn't have to go on the road over Cranbury Head. But Mum ignored our feelings and put on her brave and merry manner that annoys Chris so much, and off we drove. Chris and I tried not to look at the pale new section of fence on the cliff top, and I think Mum tried, too, but we could *sort of* see it even when we weren't looking. There's a big gap in the trees and bushes there, because it's not quite spring yet and no leaves have hidden the place. Dad must have swooped right across the road from left to right. I wondered how he felt, in that last second or so, when he knew he was going over, but I didn't say so. We were all pretending we hadn't noticed the place.

Aunt Maria's house failed to cheer us up. It's quite old, in a street of other old houses, which look very picturesque, all in shades of cream-color, and it's not very big. It looks bigger inside—almost grand and imposing. It must be the big dark furniture. All the rooms seem dark, somehow, and it smells of the way your mouth tastes when you wake up to find you've got a cold. Mum hasn't admitted to the smell, but she keeps saying she can't understand why the house is so dark. "Perhaps if she put up cheerful curtains," she says, "or moved the furniture round. The house must get quite a lot of sun through the garden at the back."

Aunt Maria greeted us with the news that Lavinia's mother was ill and Lavinia had gone to look after her. "It doesn't matter," she said, stumping toward us with two sticks. "Chris can have the little room now. I can manage quite well if somebody helps me wash and dress, and I'm sure you won't mind doing the cooking, will you, Betty, dear?"

Mum of course said she'd help in any way she could.

"Well, so you should," Aunt Maria said. "You're not at work at the moment, are you?"

I think even Mum privately found this a bit much, but she smiled and put it down to Aunt Maria being old. Mum keeps doing that. She points out that Aunt Maria was brought up in the days of servants and does not realize quite what she's asking sometimes. Chris and I suspect that Aunt Maria no sooner knew we were coming than she gave Lavinia a holiday. Chris says Lavinia was probably going to give notice. He says anyone who has to live with Aunt Maria is bound to want to leave after an hour.

"We don't need to have supper," Aunt Maria said. "I just have a glass of milk and a piece of cheese."

Mum saw our faces. "We can go out and find some fish and chips," she said.

"*What*?! In *Cranbury*!" said Aunt Maria, as if Mum had offered to go and carve up a missionary or the postman. Then she hemmed and hawed and said if poor Betty was tired after the journey and didn't want to cook, she thought there *was* a fish stall of some kind down on the seafront. "Though I expect it'll be closed at this season," she said.

Chris went off into the dusk to look, muttering things. He came back in half an hour looking windblown and told us that everything by the pier was shut. "And doesn't look as if it had ever been open in the last hundred years," he said. "Now what?"

"What a good boy you are to look after us all like this," said Aunt Maria. "I think there were some nut cutlets Lavinia put somewhere."

"I'm not a good boy, I'm hungry," said Chris. "Where are the beastly nut cutlets?"

"Christian!" said Mum.

We went and searched the kitchen. There were two nut cutlets and some eggs and things, but there was only one saucepan and a very small frying pan and almost nothing else. Mum wondered how Lavinia managed. I thought she may have taken all the cooking things with her when she went. Anyway, we invented a sort of nut scrambled eggs on toast. When I set the table, Aunt Maria said, "We're just camping out tonight. Don't bother to put napkins, dear. It's fun using kitchen cutlery."

I thought she meant it, so I didn't look for napkins until Mum whispered, "Don't be *silly,* Mig! It's just her polite way of saying she's used to napkins and her best silver. Go and look."

Mum is very good at understanding Aunt Maria's polite way of saying things. It has already caused her a lot of work. If she doesn't watch out, she's not going to get any kind of holiday at all. It has caused her to clean the cutlery with silver polish and to roll up the hall carpet in case someone slips on it in the night, and put the potted plants in the bath, and force Chris to wind all seven clocks, and help Aunt Maria upstairs, where Mum and I undressed her and put her hair in pigtails, and plump her pillows in the way Aunt Maria said she wouldn't bother with as Lavinia was not there, and then to lay out her things for morning. Aunt Maria said we were not to, of course.

"And I won't bother with breakfast, now Lavinia's not here to bring it me in bed, dear," was Aunt Maria's final demand. Mum promised to bring her breakfast on a tray at eight-thirty sharp. It's a very useful way of bullying people. I went downstairs and tried it on Chris.

"You don't need to bother to bring the cases in from the car," I told him. "We're camping on the floor in our clothes!"

"Oh!" said Chris. "I forgot the damn cases . . . " And he had jumped up to fetch them before he realized I was laughing. He was just deciding whether to laugh or to snarl, when there was a hullabaloo from Aunt Maria upstairs. Mum, who was halfway down, went charging up in a panic, thinking she had fallen out of bed.

"When Lavinia's here, I always get her to turn the gas and electricity off at ten o'clock sharp," Aunt Maria shouted. "But you can leave it on since you're my visitors."

As a result of this, I am writing this by candlelight. Mum is on the other side of the candle, making a huge list of all the things we are going to buy for Aunt Maria tomorrow. Reading upside down I can see *saucepans* and *potatoes* and *fish slice* and *pruning shears*. Mum's obviously been not-asked to do some gardening, too.

We kept the electricity on until ten-fifteen, in fact, so that we could see to get settled into our rooms. Chris's little room is halfway up the stairs and full of books. I feel envious. I don't mind sharing with Mum of course, but the bed is not very big and the room is still full of Lavinia's things. As Mum said, rather wryly, Lavinia obviously couldn't wait to get away. Her cupboard and drawers are full of clothes. She has left silver-backed brushes on the dressing table and slippers under the bed, and Mum has got all worried about not making a mess of her things. She has moved the silver brushes and the silver-framed photograph of Lavinia and her mother to a high shelf. Lavinia is one of those people who always looks old. I remember thinking she was about ninety when I last came here when I was little. In the photo, Lavinia and her mother might be twins, two old ladies smiling away. One is labeled "Mother" and one "Me," so they can't be twins.

Then at nearly ten-fifteen, when Mum was taking the potted plants out of the bath in order to make Chris get into it for what Chris calls washing and I call wallowing in his own mud, someone hammered at the back door. Chris opened it as Mum and I came running. A lady stood there beaming a great torch at us. She was Mum's age—or maybe younger: you know how hard it is to tell—and she had a crisp, clean, nunlike look.

"You must be Betty Laker," she said to Mum. "I'm Elaine. From next door," she added, when she saw that meant nothing. And she marched past Chris and me without noticing us. "I brought this torch," she explained, "because I thought you would have turned the electricity off by now. She insists on it. She worries about fires in the night."

"Chris," said Mum. "Find out where the switch is."

"It's behind the door here," said Elaine. "Turn it off when I've gone. I'll only stay a moment to make sure you know what needs doing. We're all so glad you could come and look after her. Any problems up to now?"

"No," said Mum, looking a bit dazed.

Elaine strolled past us into the dining room where she sauntered here and there, swinging the big torch and looking at Mum's knitting and my notebooks and Chris's homework piled on various chairs. She was wearing a crisply belted black mackintosh raincoat and she was very thin. I wondered if she was a policewoman. "She likes the place tidier than this," Elaine said.

"We're in the middle of unpacking," Mum said humbly. Chris looked daggers. He hates Mum crawling to people.

Elaine gave Mum a smile. It put two matching creases on either side of her mouth, but it was not what I would call a real smile. Funny, because she was quite pretty, really. "You've gathered that she needs dressing, undressing, washing, and her cooking done," she said. "The three of you can probably bathe her, can't you? Good. And when you want to take her for some air, I'll bring the wheelchair round. It lives at my house because there's more room. And do be careful she doesn't fall over. I expect you'll manage. We'll all be dropping in to see how you're getting on, anyway. So . . . " She looked round again. "I'll love you and leave you," she said. She shot Chris, for some reason, another of her strange smiles and marched off again, calling over her shoulder, "Don't forget the electricity."

"She gives her orders!" Chris said. "Mum, did you know what we were in for? If you didn't, we've been got on false pretenses."

"I know, but Aunt Maria *does* need help," Mum said helplessly. "Where's that electricity switch? And are there any candles?"

There were two candles. Mum added *candles* to her list before she got into bed just now. Now she's sitting there saying, "These sheets aren't very clean. I must wash them tomorrow. She's not got a washing machine but there must be a launderette somewhere in the place." Then she went on to, "Mig, you've written *reams*. Stop and come to bed now or there won't be any of that notebook left." She was beginning on "There won't be any of that candle left, either—" when Chris came storming in wearing just his pants.

He said, "I don't know what this is. It was under my pillow." He threw something stormily on the floor and went away again.

It is pink and frilly and called St. Margaret. We think it is probably Lavinia's nightdress. Mum has spent the last quarter of an hour marveling about it. "She must have been called away in a hurry, after all," she said, preparing to have more agonies of guilt. "She'd already moved down to the little room to make room for us. Oh, I feel awful!"

"Mum," I said, "if you can feel awful looking at someone's old nightie, what are you going to feel if you happen to see Chris's socks?" That made her laugh. She's forgotten to feel guilty now and she's threatening to blow out the candle.

two

There is a ghost in Chris's room.

I wrote that two days ago. Since then events have moved so fast that snails are whizzing by, blurred with speed. I am paralyzed with boredom, Mum has knitted three sleeves for one sweater for the same reason, and Chris is behaving worse and worse. So is Aunt Maria. We all hate Elaine and the other Mrs. Urs.

How can Aunt Maria bear living in Cranbury with no television? The days have all gone the same way, starting with Mum leaping out of bed and waking me up in her hurry to get breakfast as soon as Aunt Maria begins thumping her stick on the floor. While I'm getting up, Aunt Maria is sounding off next door. "No, no, dear. It's quite fun to eat runny egg for a change—I usually tell Lavinia to do them for five and a half minutes, but it doesn't matter a bit." That was the last two days. Today Mum must have got the egg right, because Aunt Maria was on about how interesting to eat flabby toast, dear. The noise wakes Chris up and he comes forth like the skeleton in the cupboard. Snarl, snarl!

Chris is not usually like this. The first morning, I asked him what was the matter and he said, "Oh, nothing. There's a ghost in my room." The second morning he wouldn't speak. Today I didn't speak, either.

Mum has just time to drink a cup of coffee before Aunt Maria is thumping her stick again, for us to get her up. We have to hook her into a corset thing which is like shiny pink armor, and you should just see her knickers. Chris did. He said they would make good trousers for an Arabian dancing girl, provided the girl was six feet tall and highly respectable. I thought of Aunt Maria with a jewel in her tummy button and was nearly sick laughing. Aunt Maria made me worse by saying, "I have a great sense of humor, dears. Tell me the joke." That was while Chris and I were helping her downstairs. She was in full regalia by then, in a tweed suit and two necklaces, and Mum was trying to make Aunt Maria's bed the way Lavinia is supposed-to-do-it-but-it-doesn't-matter-dear.

She comes and sits in state in the living room then. It is somehow the darkest room in the house, though sun streams in from the brown garden. One of us has to sit there with her. We found that out the first day when we were all getting ready to go shopping for the things on Mum's huge list. Chris was saying sarcastically that he couldn't wait to see some of the hot spots in town, when Aunt Maria caught up with what we were talking about.

She said, in her special urgent scandalized way, "You're not going *out*!"

"Yes," said Chris. "We are on holiday, you know."

Mum shut him up by saying, "*Christian!*" and explained about the shopping.

"But suppose I fall!" said Aunt Maria. "Suppose someone calls. How shall I answer the door?"

"You opened the door to us when we came," I said.

Aunt Maria promptly went all gentle and martyred and said none of us knew what it was like to be old, and did we realize she sometimes never saw a soul for a whole month on end? "You go, dears. Get your fresh air," she said.

Naturally Mum got guilty at that, and, just as naturally, it was me that had to stay behind. I spent the next three hundred hours sitting in a little brown chair facing Aunt Maria. She sits on a yellow brocade sofa with knobs on and silk ropes hooked around the knobs to stop the sofa's arms falling down. Her feet are plonked on the wine-colored carpet and her hands are plonked on her sticks. Aunt Maria is a heavy sort of lady. I keep thinking of her as huge and I keep being surprised to find that she is nothing like as tall as Chris, and not even as tall as Mum. I think she may only be as tall as me. But her character is enormous—right up to the ceiling.

She talks. It is all about her friends in Cranbury. "Corinne West and Adele Taylor told Zoe Green—Zoe Green has a brilliant mind, dear: she's read every book in the library—and Zoe Green told Hester Bailey—Hester paints charming watercolors, all real scenes, everyone says she's as good as van Gogh—and Hester said I was quite right to be hurt at what Miss Phelps had been saying. After all I'd done for Miss Phelps! I used to send Lavinia over to her, but I wonder if I should anymore. We told Benita Wallins, and she said on no account. Selma Tidmarsh had told her all Miss Phelps had said. Selma and Phyllis—Phyllis Forbes, that is, not Phyllis West—wanted to go round and speak to Miss Phelps, but I said 'No, I shall turn the other cheek.' So Phyllis West went to Ann Haversham and said . . . "

On and on. You end up feeling you are in a sort of bubble filled with that getting-a-cold smell, and inside that bubble is Cranbury and Aunt Maria, and that is the entire world. It is hard to remember there is any land outside Cranbury. I got into a kind of daze of boredom. It was humming in my ears. When you get that way, the most ordinary things get violently exciting. I know when I looked round and saw a cat on the living room windowsill, it was like Christmas or my birthday or when Chris's friend Andy notices me. Wonderful! And it was one of those gray, fluffy cats with a flat, silly face that are normally utterly boring. It was staring intensely in at us through the glass, opening its mouth and dribbling down its gray ruff, and I stared back into its flat yellow eyes—they were slightly crossed—as if that cat was my favorite friend in all the world.

"You're not attending, dear," said Aunt Maria, and she turned to see what I was staring at. Her face went red. She levered herself up on one stick and stumped toward the window, slashing the air with her other stick. "Get off! How dare you sit on my windowsill!" The cat glared in stupid horror and fled for its life. Aunt Maria sat back down, puffing. "He comes in my garden all the time," she said. "After birds. As I was saying, Ann Haversham and Rosa Brisling were great friends until Miss Phelps said that. Now you mustn't think I'm annoyed with Amaryllis Phelps, but I was hurt—"

I thought she was horrid to that cat. I couldn't listen to her after that. I sat and wondered about Chris's ghost. It could have been a joke. But if it wasn't—I didn't know whether I wanted it to be Dad's ghost trying to tell Chris where his body was, or not. The idea made my teeth want to chatter, and I had a sort of ache of fear and excitement.

"Do attend, dear," said Aunt Maria. "This is interesting."

"I am," I said. She had been talking about Elaine-next-door. I had sort of heard. "We met Elaine," I said. "She came in last night with a torch."

"*You* mustn't call her Elaine, dear," Aunt Maria said. "She's Mrs. Blackwell."

"Why not?" I said. "She said Elaine."

"That's because I always call her that," Aunt Maria said. "But if you do, it's rude."

So I'm calling her Elaine. Elaine came marching in again, in her black mac but without her torch, at the same time as Chris and Mum. I'd heard Chris's voice and then Mum's and I jumped up, feeling I was being let out of prison. Something was actually happening! Then the living room door opened and it was Elaine. "Don't go, dear," Aunt Maria said to me. "I want you here to be introduced."

I had to stand there, while Elaine took no notice of me, as before. She went to Aunt Maria and kissed her cheek. "They've done your shopping," she said, "and I told them where to put things. Is there anything else you want me to tell them?"

"They're being very good," Aunt Maria said. She had gone all merry. "They're trying quite hard. I don't expect them to get anything right straight away."

"I see," said Elaine. "I'll go and tell them to make an effort then." She was not joking. She was like a police chief taking her orders from the Great Dictator.

"Before you do," Aunt Maria said merrily, "I want you to meet my new little Naomi. Such a dear little great-niece!"

Elaine turned her face toward me. "Mig," I said. "I prefer being called Mig."

"Hello, Naomi," said Elaine, and she strode out of the room again. When I went after her, I found her standing over Mum and Chris and scads of grocery bags, saying, "And you really must make sure she is never left alone."

Mum, looking very flustered, said, "We left Mig here."

"I know," Elaine said grimly, meaning that was what she was complaining of. Then she turned to Chris. Her mouth made the stretch with two creases at the ends. "You," she said. "You have the look of a gallant young man. I'm sure you'll keep your aunt company in future, won't you?"

We think it was meant to be flirtatious. We stared at one another as the back door shut crisply behind Elaine. "Well!" Mum said. "You seem to have made a hit, Chris! And talking of hits, hit her I shall if she gives me one more order. Who does she think she is?"

"Aunt Maria's chief of police," I said.

"Right!" said Mum.

Then we unpacked all the loads of provisions, and guess what? We found a deep freeze in the cupboard beside the sink, absolutely stuffed with food. There was ice cream and bread and hot dogs and raspberries in it. Half the stuff Mum had bought was things that were there already. Chris sorted through it with great zeal. Mum is always amazed at how much he eats and keeps saying, "You *can't* still be hungry!" I have tried to explain, from my own experience. It's a sort of nagging need you have, even when you feel full. It's not starving, just that you keep wanting more to eat.

"Yes," says Mum. "That's what I mean. How can you find room? Oh, dear. We wronged poor Lavinia again. She left Aunt Maria very well supplied, after all."

Chris taxed Aunt Maria with this over lunch. Aunt Maria said loftily, "I never pry into the kitchen, dear. But frozen food is very bad for you." And before Chris could point out that Aunt Maria was at that moment eating frozen peas, Aunt Maria rounded on Mum. "I was so ashamed, dear, when Elaine came in. The thought of her seeing you and Naomi in that state. And you went *out* like that, dear."

"What state? Out like what?" we all said.

Aunt Maria lowered her eyes. "In trousers!" she whispered, hushed and horrified. Mum and I stared from Mum's jeans to mine and then at one another. "And Naomi's hair so untidy," Aunt Maria continued. "She must have forgotten to plait it today. But of course you'll both change this afternoon, won't you? In case any of my friends call."

"And what about me?" Chris asked sweetly. "Shall I wear a skirt, too?" Aunt Maria pretended not to hear, so he added, "In case any of your friends call?"

"These peas are really delicious," Aunt Maria said

loudly to Mum. "I wouldn't have thought peas were in season yet. Where did you find them?"

"They're frozen," Chris said, even louder, but she pretended not to hear that, either.

It is very hard to know how deaf Aunt Maria is. Sometimes she seems like a post, like then, and sometimes she can sit in the living room and hear what you whisper in the kitchen with both doors shut in between. Chris says the rule is she hears if you don't want her to. Chris is thoroughly exasperated by that. He keeps trying to practice his guitar. In the little room halfway upstairs, with his door shut, Mum and I can hardly hear the guitar, but whenever Chris starts to play, Aunt Maria springs up, shrieking, "What's that noise? There's a burglar trying to break into the house!" I know how Chris feels, because Aunt Maria does that when I have my Walkman on, too. Even if I turn it so low hardly a whisper comes into the earphones, Aunt Maria shrieks, "What's that noise? Is the tank in the loft leaking?"

Mum has made us both stop. "It *is* her house, loves," she said when we argued. "We're only her guests."

"On a working holiday!" Chris snarled. Mum was cleaning Aunt Maria's brass, because Aunt Maria said that this was Lavinia's day for doing it, but she didn't expect Mum to do it.

On the same grounds, Mum changed into her good dress and made me wear a skirt. I pointed out I've only got one skirt with me—my pleated one—and Mum said, "Mig, I'll buy you another. We *are* her guests."

"Oh good," said Chris. "Is that a rule—visitors have to do what the owner of the house wants? Next time Andy comes round in London I'll make him kiss Mig."

That made me hit Chris, and Aunt Maria shrieked that slates were falling off the roof. "See what I mean?" said Chris. "It *is* her house. Pieces fall off if you hit me. Wicked, destructive Mig, knocking nice Auntie's house down."

I think he meant me to laugh, but Aunt Maria was getting me down, too, so I didn't. I stopped talking to Chris for a while. What with that, and being numbed with boredom, I didn't manage to speak sensibly to Chris until two whole days later. It was silly. I kept wanting to ask him about his ghost, and I didn't.

In the afternoons, Aunt Maria's friends all come. They are the ones she talks about all morning. I had expected them all to be old hags, but they are quite ordinary ladies, mostly in smart clothes and smart hairdos. Some of them are even nearly young, like Elaine. Corinne West and Adele Taylor, who came first, are Elaine-aged and stylish. Benita Wallins, who came with them, was more the sort I'd expected, stumping along with bandages under her stockings, in a hat and a shiny quilted coat. From the greedy interested looks she gave us, you could see she knew we'd be there and couldn't wait to inspect us. They are all Mrs. Something and we are supposed to call them that. Chris calls them all Mrs. Ur and mixes their names up on purpose.

Anyway, they came and Mum made them all mugs of coffee. Aunt Maria gave a merry laugh. "We're camping out at the moment, Corinne, dear. Now this is Betty and Chris, and I want you all to meet my niece, my dear little Naomi." She always says that, and it makes me want to be rude like Chris, only I can never think of things to say until after they've gone. I am a failure and a hypocrite, because I feel just as rude as Chris. But it just doesn't come out.

They must have gone straight next door when they left. Elaine marched in ten minutes later, using her two-line smile and uttering steely laughs. When Elaine laughs, it is like the biggest of Aunt Maria's clocks striking—a running-down whir, followed by clanging. We think this means that Elaine is being social and diplomatic. She flings her hair back across the shoulders of her black mac and corners Mum. "You'll have a lot of hurt feelings," she said, "if you give any of the others coffee in mugs."

"Oh? What should I do then?" Mum asked, making an effort to stand up to Elaine.

"I advise you to find the silver teapot and her best china," Elaine said. "And some cake if you've got it. You know how polite she is. She'd sit there dying of shame rather than tell you herself." She shot out the two-line smile again. "Just a hint. I'll let myself out," she said, and went.

"Doesn't she ever wear anything but that black mac?" Chris asked loudly as the back door clicked shut. "Perhaps she grows it, like skin."

We all hoped Elaine had heard. But as usual she had conquered. Mum got out best tea things when Hester Bailey and three Mrs. Urs turned up soon after that. Aunt Maria would not let me help because she wanted to introduce her "dear little Naomi," and when Chris tried to help, Aunt Maria said it was woman's work. "I don't trust him with my best china," she added in a loud whisper to Phyllis Forbes and the other Mrs. Urs. Mum ran about frantically, and Chris seethed. I had to sit and listen to Hester Bailey, who was actually quite sensible and nice-seeming. We talked about pictures and painting and how horribly impossible it is to paint water.

"Particularly the sea," Hester Bailey said. "That bit when the tide is coming up over the sand, all transparent, with lacy edges."

I was saying how right she was, when Aunt Maria's voice cut across everything. How can Elaine think Aunt Maria would rather die of shame than say anything?

"Oh, dear! I do apologize," Aunt Maria shouted. "This is *bought cake*."

"Oh, horrors!" Chris promptly said from the other side of the room. "Mum paid for it herself, too, so we're all eating pound notes."

Poor Mum. She glared at Chris and then tried to apologize, but Selma Tidmarsh and the other Mrs. Urs all began shouting that it tasted very wholesome, it was very *good* for a bought cake, while Aunt Maria pushed her plate aside and turned her head away from it. And Hester Bailey said to me, "Or a wave, with green shadows and foam on it," just as if nothing had happened at all. She gave me a book when she got up to go. "I brought it for you," she said. "It's the kind of pictures a little girl like you will love."

"I'm sorry," Mum said to Aunt Maria after they'd all left.

I think she was meaning she was sorry about Chris, but Aunt Maria said, "It's all right, dear. I expect Lavinia has put the baking tins in an unexpected place. You'll have found them by tomorrow."

For a moment I thought Mum was going to explode. But she took a deep breath and went out into the rain and the wind to garden. I could see her savagely pruning roses, *snip-chop,* as if each twig was one of Aunt Maria's fingers, while I put Hester Bailey's book on the table and started to look at it.

Oh, dear. I think Hester Bailey may be as dotty as Zoe Green underneath. Or she doesn't know better. Mostly the pictures were of fairies, little flittery ones, or sweet-faced maidens in bonnets, but there were some that were so queer and peculiar that they did things to my stomach. There was a street of people who looked as if their faces had melted, and two at least of woodlands, where the trees seemed to have leering faces and nightmare twiggy hands. And there was one called "A naughty little girl is punished" that was worst of all. It was all dark except for the girl, so you couldn't quite see *what* was doing it to her, but her bright clear figure was being pushed underground by something on top of her, and something else had her long hair and was pulling her under, and there were these black whippy things, too. She looked terrified, and no wonder.

"Charming!" Chris said, dropping crumbs over my shoulder as he ate the last of the pound-note cake. "Mum's being told off again, look."

I looked out of the window into the dusk. Sure enough, Elaine was standing over Mum with her hands on the hips of her flapping black mac, and Mum was looking humble and flustered again. "Honestly—," I began.

But Aunt Maria was calling out, "What are you saying, dears? It's rude to whisper. Is it that cat again? One of you call Betty in. It's time she was cooking supper."

This is the sort of reason I never got to speak to Chris, and never got to write in my notebook, either. When I went to camp, it was more private than it is in Aunt Maria's house. But I have made a Deep Religious

Vow to write something every day now. I need to, to relieve my feelings.

The next day was the same, only that morning I went out with Mum, and Chris obeyed Elaine's orders and stayed with Aunt Maria. Would you believe this: I have still not seen the sea, except the day we came, when it was nearly dark and I was trying not to look at the piece of new fence on Cranbury Head. That morning we went round and round looking for cake tins, then up and down and out into the country behind, where it is farms and fields and woods, looking for the Laundromat. In the end Mum said she felt like a thief with loot and we had to bring the bundle of dirty sheets home again.

"Give them to me," Elaine said sternly, meeting us on the pavement outside the house. She held out a black mackintosh arm. Mum clutched the laundry defensively to her, determined not to give Elaine anything. It was ridiculous. It was only dirty sheets, after all. Elaine made her two-line smile and even laughed, a whir without the chimes! "I have a washing machine," she said.

Mum handed over the bundle and smiled, and it was almost normal.

That afternoon Zoe Green turned up for best china and cake, and so did Phyllis Whatsis and another Mrs. Ur—Rosa, I think. Mum had made a cake. Aunt Maria had spent all lunchtime telling Mum it didn't matter, to make sure Mum did, but she called out all the same while

Zoe Green was kissing her, "Have you made a cake, dear?"

Chris said loudly from his corner, "She. Has. Made. A. Cake. Or do you want me to spell it?"

Everyone pretended not to hear, which was quite easy, because Zoe Green is quite cuckoo. She runs about and gushes in a poopling sort of voice—I can imitate it by holding my tongue between my teeth while I talk. "Stho dthis iths dhear dithul Ndaombil" she pooples. "Ndow don'd dtell mbe I dlovbe guessthing. You dwere bordn in lade DNovember. DYou're Sthagittharius."

"No, she's not, she's Libra," said Chris. "I'm Leo."

But no one was listening to Chris, because Zoe Green was going on and on about horoscopes and Sagittarius, loud and long—and spitting, rather. She wears her hair in two buns, one on each ear, and long traily clothes with a patchwork jacket on top, all rather dirty. She's the only one who looks mad. I tried several times to tell her I *wasn't* born in November, but she was in an ecstasy of cusps and ruling planets, and she didn't hear.

"*Such* a dear friend," Aunt Maria said to me.

And Phyllis Ur leaned over and whispered, "We love her *so* much, dear. She's never been the same since her son—well, we won't talk about that. But she's a very valued member of Cranbury society."

They meant I was to shut up and let Z.G. go on. I

looked at Chris and he looked back and then up at the ceiling. Bonkers, he meant. Then I sat there listening and wondering how it was I never seemed to talk to Chris at the moment, when I did so want to know if he really meant that about the ghost.

Then Mum brought in the cake. Chris looked Aunt Maria in the eye and got up to pass the cake round.

Aunt Maria said, in a sad low voice, "He'll drop it."

If that wasn't the last straw to Chris, it was when Zoe Green dived forward and peered at the slice of cake he was trying to pass her. "What's in this? Ndothing I'mb adlerdjig to, I hobe?"

"I wouldn't know," Chris said. "Those things in it that look like currants are really rabbits' doo's, so if you're allergic to rabbits' doo's, don't eat it." Everyone, including Zoe Green, stared, and then began to try to pretend he hadn't said it. But Chris seized a cup of tea and held that out, too. "How about some horse piss?" he said.

There was a gabble of people talking about something else, in the midst of which Mum said, "Christian, I'll—" Unfortunately, I'd just taken a mouthful of tea. I choked, and had to go out into the kitchen to cough over the sink. Through my coughings, I heard Chris's voice again. Very loud.

"That's right. Pretend I didn't say it! Or why not say, 'He's only an adolescent, and he's upset because his father fell off Cranbury Head'? He did, you know. Squish."

Then I heard the door slam behind him.

Outcry. It was awful. Aunt Maria was having a screaming fit, Zoe Green was hooting like an owl. I could hear Mum crying. It was so awful I stayed in the kitchen. And it went on being so awful, I was coughing my way to the back door to get right away like Chris had, when it shot open and Elaine strode in, black mac and all.

"I'll have to have a word with that brother of yours," she said. "Where is he?"

All I can think of is that she has a radio link between her house and this one. How could she have known? I mean, she may have heard the noise, but how could she have known it was Chris? I stared at her clean, stern face. She has awfully fanatical eyes, I couldn't help noticing. "I don't know," I said. "Outside somewhere, probably."

"Then I'll go and look for him," Elaine said. She went out through the door and said over her shoulder, "If I can't find him, tell him from me he's riding for a fall. Really. It's serious."

I wish she hadn't said, "riding for a fall." Not those words.

When the noise quieted down, I went back to the dining room. Both the Mrs. Urs patted my arm and said, "There, there, dear." They seem to think it was Chris who upset me.

three

Now I feel as guilty as Mum. It got dark, and Chris still hadn't come back. Aunt Maria was really worried about him. "Suppose he's gone down on the beach and slipped on a rock!" she kept saying. "If he's broken his leg or twisted his ankle, nobody will know. I think you ought to ring the police, dear, and not bother about getting supper."

Who needs the police, I thought, with Elaine after him? And Mum said, in the special high, cheerful voice she always uses to Aunt Maria, "Oh, he'll be all right, Auntie. Boys will be boys."

Aunt Maria refused to be comforted. She went on, low and direful, "And the pier is dangerous in the dark. Suppose the current took him. Thank goodness little Naomi is safe!"

"That makes me want to say I'm going out for a swim," I said to Mum.

"Don't you dare!" said Mum. "Chris is bad enough

without *you* starting, too."

"Then shut her up," I said.

"What's that, dear?" said Aunt Maria. "Who's shut up?"

It went on like that until the back door crashed open and Elaine marched Chris in, swinging her torch. She had hold of Chris by his shoulder, just as if she had arrested him. "Here he is," she said to Mum. "I've given him a talking to."

"Really? How very helpful you are!" Mum said, and took a quick anxious look at Chris's face. He looked almost as if he was trying not to laugh, and I could see Mum was relieved.

By then Aunt Maria cottoned on. "Oh, Elaine!" she shouted. "I've been ill with worry! Have you brought him? Where did you find him? Is he all right?"

"In the street," said Elaine. "He was on his way back here. He's fine. Aren't you, my lad?"

"Yes, apart from a squeezed shoulder," Chris retorted.

Elaine let go of Chris and pretended to hit him with her torch. "Don't let him do that again," she said to Mum. "You know how she worries."

"Stay with me, Elaine," Aunt Maria bawled. "I've had such a shock!"

"Sorry!" Elaine bawled back. "I have to get Larry his supper." And she went.

It was ages before I could ask Chris what Elaine had said to him. Aunt Maria made him sit down next to her and told him over and over again how worried she had been. She kept asking him where he had been and not giving him time to answer. Chris took it all in a humorous sort of way, so different from the way he had been before that I thought Elaine must have hit him on the head with her torch or something.

"No, she just grabbed me," Chris said. "And I said, 'Do you arrest me in the name of the law?' And she said, 'You can be as rude as you like to me, my lad. I don't mind. But I'm not having your aunt worried.'"

"What's that?" said Aunt Maria. "Who's worried?"

"Me," said Chris. "Elaine worried me like a rabbit."

"I expect Larry's been out shooting," said Aunt Maria. "He often brings home a rabbit. I wonder if he's got one for us. I'm fond of rabbit stew."

Chris looked at the ceiling and gave up. He's playing his guitar at the moment, and Aunt Maria is pretending not to hear that, either. It looks as if All is Forgiven. And that's what makes me feel guilty. Mum and I have put Aunt Maria to bed and she's sitting up on her pillows, all clean and rosy in her lacy white nightgown, with her hair in frizzy pigtails, listening to *A Book at Bedtime* on Mum's radio. She looks like a teddy bear. Quite lovable. Mum asked her to say when she wants the electricity off, and she gave the sweetest smile and said, "Oh, when you're ready. Let Naomi finish that story she's writing so busily first."

And I feel horrible. I've read through my notebook and it's full of just beastly things about Aunt Maria and she thinks I'm writing a story. It's worse than Chris, because I'm being secret in my nastiness. I wish I was charitable, like Mum. I admire Mum. She's so pretty, as well as so cheerful. She has a neat little nose and a pretty forehead that comes out in a little bulge. Her eyes always look bright, even when she's tired. Chris takes after Mum. They both have those eyes, with long curly eyelashes. I wish I did. What eyelashes I have are butterscotch-color, like my hair, and they do nothing for plain brown eyes. My forehead is straight. I am not sweet at all and I wish Aunt Maria would not keep calling me her "sweet little Naomi." I feel a real worm.

I felt so bad after that, that I just had to talk to Mum before we blew out the candle. We both sat up in bed. Mum smoked a cigarette and I cried, and we both expected Aunt Maria to wake up and shout that the house was on fire. But she didn't. We could hear her snoring, while downstairs Chris defiantly twanged away at his guitar.

"My poor Mig!" said Mum. "I know just how you feel!"

"No, you don't!" I snuffled. "You're charitable. I'm worse than Chris, even!"

"Charitable, be damned!" said Mum. "I want to slay Auntie half the time, and I could *strangle* Elaine *all* the time! At first I was as muddled as you are, because Auntie *is* very old and she can be very sweet, and I only got by because I do rather like nursing people. Then Chris did me a favor, behaving like that. He was admitting something I was pretending wasn't there. People do have savage feelings, Mig."

"But it's not *right* to have savage feelings!" I gulped.

"No, but everyone does," said Mum, lighting a second cigarette off the end of the first. "Auntie does. That's what's upsetting us all. She's utterly selfish and a complete expert in making other people do what she wants. She uses people's guilt about their savage feelings. Does that make you feel better?"

"Not really," I said. "She has to make people do things for her, because she can't do things for herself, can she?"

"As to that," Mum said, puffing away, "I'm not convinced, Mig. I've been looking at her carefully, and I don't think there's too much wrong with her. I think she could do a lot more for herself if she wanted to. I think she's just convinced herself she can't. Tomorrow I'm going to have a go at making her do some things for herself."

That made me feel better. I think it made Mum feel better, too, but she hasn't made much headway getting

Aunt Maria to do things. She's been trying half the morning. Aunt Maria will say, "I left my spectacles on the sideboard, but it doesn't matter, dear."

"Off you go and get them," Mum says, in a cheerful loud voice.

There is a pause, then Aunt Maria utters in a reproachful gentle groan, "I'm getting old, dear."

"You can try, at least," Mum says encouragingly.

"Suppose I fall," suggests Aunt Maria.

"Yes, do," says Chris. "Fall on your face and give us all a good laugh." Mum glares at him and I go and find the spectacles. That's the way it was until the gray cat suddenly put in an appearance, mewing through the window at us with its ugly flat face almost pressed against the glass. Mum is right. Aunt Maria jumped up with no trouble at all and practically ran to the window, slashing the air with both sticks and shouting at the cat to go away. It fled.

"What did you do that for?" Chris said.

"I'm not having him in my garden," Aunt Maria said. "He eats birds."

"Who does he belong to?" Mum asked. She likes cats as much as I do.

"How should I know?" said Aunt Maria. She was so annoyed with the cat that she took herself back to the sofa without remembering to use her sticks once. Mum raised her eyebrows and looked at me. See? Then we unwisely left Chris indoors and went out to look for the cat in the garden. We didn't find it, but when we got back Chris was simmering. Aunt Maria was giving him a gentle talking-to. "It doesn't matter about *me,* dear, but my friends were so distressed. Promise me you'll never speak like that again."

Chris no doubt deserved it, but Mum said hastily, "Chris and Mig, I'm going to pack you a lunch and you're going to go out for some fresh air. You're to stay out all afternoon."

"All afternoon!" cried Aunt Maria. "But I have my Circle of Healing here this afternoon. It will do the children such a lot of good to come to the meeting."

"Fresh air will do them more good," said Mum. "Chris looks pale." Which was true. Chris looked as if he hadn't slept much. He was white and getting one or two pimples again. Mum took no notice of Aunt Maria's protests—it was windy, it was going to rain, we would get wet—and bullied us out of the house with warm clothes and a bag of food. "Do me a favor and try to enjoy yourselves for a change," she said.

"But what about you?" I said.

"I'll be fine. I shall do some gardening while she has her meeting," Mum said.

We went out into the street. "She's martyring herself," I said. "I wish she wouldn't."

Chris said, "She needs to work off her guilt about

Dad. Let her be, Mig." He smiled in his normal understanding way. He seemed to go back to his old self as soon as we were in the street. "Shall I tell you something I noticed about this street yesterday? See that house opposite?"

He pointed, and I said, "Yes," and looked. And the lace curtains in the front window of the house twitched as somebody hastily got back from them. Otherwise it was a little cream-colored house as gloomy as the rest of the street, with a large twelve on its front door.

"Number twelve," said Chris as we walked on up the street. "The only house in this street with a number, Mig, apart from twenty-two down the other end on the same side. That means odd numbers on Aunt Maria's side, doesn't it? And that makes Aunt Maria's house number thirteen whichever way you count the houses."

Chris is always thinking about numbers, normally. This proved he was back to normal. I said it *would* be number thirteen, and we laughed as we walked down to the seafront. It was very windy and quite deserted there, but very respectable somehow. Chris shouted that even the concrete sheds were tasteful. They were. We went past the kiddies' bathing pool and the tame little place with swings, and along the front. The tide was in. Waves came spouting up against the seawall, gray and violent, sending water bashing across the path. Our feet got wet and the noise was so huge that we talked in shouts and licked salt off our mouths afterward. There was only one other person out that we saw, the whole length of the bay, and he was right at the beginning—an elderly gent huddled in a tweed coat, who tried to raise his tweed hat politely to us; but he only put a hand to it, in case it got blown away.

"Morning!" we shouted. He shouted, "Afternoon!" Very correct. It was after midday. Only *I* always think afternoon begins when you've had lunch, and we hadn't yet.

When we were near the pier, I shouted to Chris, "The ghost in your room—is it a he or a she?" It was a bad place to ask important things. The sea was crashing and sucking round the iron girders, and the buildings on the pier kept cutting the wind off, so that we were in a nest of quiet one moment, all warm with our ears ringing, and then out again into icy noise.

"A man!" yelled Chris. "And it's not Dad," he said, as we went into a nest of quiet. "I saw you thinking it might be and it's not. It's ever such a strange-looking fellow, like a cross between a court jester and a parrot."

The wind howled and I didn't hear straight. "A *pirate*?" I shouted.

"*Parrot!*" Chris screamed. And I think what he shouted after that was "Pretty Polly! Long John Silver! I am the ghost of Able Mable! Parrot cage on table!"

Shouting in the wind makes you shout silly things

anyway, and I think Chris was shouting in order not to be scared. Anyway, I got in a real muddle and I thought he was trying to tell me the ghost's name. "Neighbor?" I yelled. "John?"

"What do you mean, Neighbor John?" howled Chris.

"The ghost's name. Is it Neighbor John?" I screeched.

By the time we got into a pocket of quiet again and sorted out what we both thought we were saying, we were in fits of laughter and Neighbor John seemed a good name for the ghost. So we call him that now. I keep thinking of Chris seeing a large red pirate parrot, and then I remember he said, "court jester," too, so I correct the red parrot into one of those white ones with a yellow crest that are really cockatoos. I think their crests look like jester's caps, and ghosts should be white. But I just can't imagine a *man* looking like that. Chris told me more about the ghost at intervals all through the day. I think he was glad to have someone to tell. But I know there were things he didn't tell, and I keep wondering why, and what they were.

He said he woke up suddenly the first night, thinking he'd forgotten to blow out the candle. But then he realized it was light coming in from a streetlight somewhere. He could see a man outlined against the window, bent over with his back to Chris. The man seemed to be hunting for something in one of the bookcases.

"So I called out to him," said Chris.

"Weren't you scared?" I said. My heart seemed to be beating in my throat at just the idea. "Yes, but I thought he was a burglar then," Chris said. "I sat up and thought about people getting killed for surprising burglars and decided I'd pretend I was sleeping with a gun under my pillow. So I said, 'Put your hands up and turn round.' And he whirled round and stared at me. He looked absolutely astonished—as if he hadn't realized there was anyone else there—and we sort of stared at each other for a while. By that time I knew he wasn't a burglar, somehow. He had the wrong look on his face. I mean, I know he was odd-looking, but it wasn't a burglar look. I even almost knew he had lost something that belonged to him and he was looking for it because he thought it was in that room. So I said, 'What have you lost?' and he didn't answer. There was a look on his face as if he was going to speak, but he didn't."

Chris said he still didn't realize the man was a ghost, even then. At first he said he only realized next morning when he snapped at me there was a ghost in his room. Then he said, no, he must have known the moment the man turned round. The room was full of an odd feeling, he said. Then he corrected himself again. I think ghosts must be muddling things to meet. He said he began to be puzzled when he noticed the man was wearing a peculiar dark green robe, all torn and covered with mud.

By the time Chris had told me that far, we had got

right along the seafront, past all the little boats pulled up on a concrete slope, almost to Cranbury Head. We looked up the great tall pinkish cliff. It looked almost like a house, because creepers grow up it. We could just see the gap in the creepers and a glimpse of the new fence. And we both went very matter-of-fact, somehow.

Chris said, "You can see some of the rocks at the bottom, even with the tide in."

"Yes, but it was at night," I said. "They didn't see the car till morning."

Then Chris wondered how they got the car cleared away. He thought they winched it up the cliffs. I said it was easier to put it on a raft and float it to the concrete slope. "Or drag it round the sands at low tide," Chris agreed. "Poor old car."

We turned and went back through the town then. I kept thinking of the car. I know it so well. It was our family car until six months ago, when Dad took a lady called Verena Bland to France in it and phoned to say he wasn't coming back. I wondered if the car still had the messy place on the backseat where I knelt on an egg while I was fighting with Chris. Does seawater wash out egg? And I remembered again that I'd left the story I was writing in that hiding hole under the dashboard. All washed out with seawater. I hated to think of that car smelling of sea and rust. It used to have a smell of its own. Dad once got into the wrong car by accident and knew it was wrong by the smell. Chris didn't get on with Dad. I did, a lot of the time, unless Dad was in a really foul mood.

"When *did* you know it was a ghost then?" I said.

"Right at the end, I suppose," Chris said. "He didn't speak, but he gave a great mischievous sort of smile. And while I was wondering what was so funny, I realized I could see books in the shelf through him and he was sort of fading out."

That makes four different versions, I thought. "Weren't you frightened?"

"Not so much as I expected," Chris said. "I quite liked him."

"And has he come every night?" I asked.

"Yes," said Chris. "I keep asking him what he wants, and he always seems to be just going to tell me, but he never does."

It was windy among the houses, too, cream houses, pink houses, tall gray houses with boards saying bed and breakfast creaking in the wind, and sand racing across the roads like running water. The place had been deserted up to then, but after that we kept meeting Mrs. Urs. We saw Benita Wallins first, puffily shaking a rug out of the front door of a B-and-B house. She shouted, "Hello, dears." Then there was Corinne West, coming round a corner with a shopping basket, Selma Tidmarsh in the next street with a scarf over her head, and Ann

Haversham walking a dog round the corner from that. It was, "Hello, how are you? Is your aunt well?" each time.

"Aunt Maria will be able to plot our course exactly at this rate," I said. "Or Elaine will. How many more of them?"

"Nine," said Chris. "She talks about thirteen Mrs. Urs. I read a book and counted while she was talking yesterday."

"Only if you count Miss Phelps and Lavinia, too," I said. "What *did* Miss Phelps say to upset her? Did she tell you?"

"No. Unless it was, 'Stop that boring yakking,'" Chris said. "Let's get on a bus and get out of this place."

But the buses don't start until next month. We went to the railway station and asked. A porter in big rubber boots told us it was out of season, but we could get a train to Aytham Junction, and it turned out that we hadn't got enough money for that. So we walked out along the path that started by the station car park, through brown plowed fields to the woods.

"I think it was the day after that I noticed mud on his robes," Chris said, looking at the plowed earth. He kept talking about the ghost like that, in snatches. "And the light seems to come with him. I experimented. I went to bed without a candle last night and I could hardly see to find the bed."

"Do you wake up each time?" I said.

"The first two nights. Last night I stayed awake to see if I could catch him appearing." Chris yawned. "I heard the clock strike three and then I must have dropped off. He was just there suddenly, and I heard four strike around the time he faded out."

We had lunch in the woods. They were good, lots of little trees all bent the same way by the sea wind. Their trunks grow in twists from all the bending they get. It gives the wood a goblin sort of look, but as soon as you are among the goblin trees you can't see any open land outside. We nearly got lost later because of that.

"But what's the ghost looking for?" I said. I know that was during lunch because I could hear the twisted trees creaking while I said it, and I remember dead leaves under my knees, clean and cold as an animal's nose.

"I'd love to know," Chris said. "I've looked all along the books in that wall. I took them out and looked behind them, in case the ghost hadn't the strength to move them, but it's just wall behind them."

"Perhaps it's a book?" I suggested. "Are any of them *A History of Hauntings*, or maybe *Dead Men of Cranbury* to give you a clue who he is?"

"No way!" said Chris. *"The Works of Balzac, The Works of Scott, Ruskin's Writings*, and *Collected Works of Joseph Conrad."* He thought a bit and the trees creaked a bit, and then he said, "I think the ghost brings rather awful dreams, but I can't remember what they are."

"How *can* you like him then?" I cried out, shuddering.

"Because the dreams are not his fault," Chris said. "You'd know if you saw him. You'd be sorry for him. You're the soft-hearted one, not me."

I do feel quite sorry for the ghost, anyway, not being able to lie quiet because he'd lost something and having to get up out of his grave every night to hunt for it. I wondered how long he'd been doing it. I asked Chris if he could tell from the ghost's clothes how long ago he died, but Chris said he never saw them clearly enough.

The creaking of the trees was making me shudder by then. I couldn't finish my lunch—Mum always gives you far too much, anyway. Chris said he was blowed if he was going to cart a bag full of half-eaten pork pie about and I hate carrying bags. So Chris put some of the cake in his pocket for later and we pushed the bag under the twisted roots of the nearest tree. Litter fiends, we are. The wood was wonderfully clear and airy, with a fresh mossy smell to it. It made it seem cleaner still that there were no leaves on the bent branches—barely even buds. We both felt ashamed of leaving the bag and made jokes about it. Chris said a passing badger would be grateful for the pork pie.

It was after that that we got lost. The wood went steeply up and steeply down. We never saw the fields, or even the sea, and we didn't know where we were until I realized that the wind always comes in from the sea. So in order to find Cranbury again we had to face into the wind. We might have been wandering all night if we hadn't done that. I said it was a witch-wood and trying to keep us forever. Chris said, "Don't be silly!" But I think he was quite scared, too: it was all so empty and so twisted. Anyway, I think what we must have done was to go right up the valley behind Cranbury and then along the hill on the other side. When we finally came steeply down and saw Cranbury below us, we were right on the opposite hill from Cranbury Head, and Cranbury was looking like half-circles of dollhouses arranged round a gray misty nothing that was the sea.

I thought it looked quite pretty from there. Chris said, "How on earth did we cross the railway? It comes right through the valley."

I don't know how we did, but we had. We could see the railway below us, too. The last big house in Cranbury was half hidden by the hill we were on, quite near the railway. We took it as a landmark and went down straight toward it. By this time it was just *beginning* to be evening, not dark yet, but sort of quietly dimming so that everything was pale and chilly. I kept telling myself this was why everything felt so strange. There was a steep field first of very wet grass. The wind had dropped. The big house was all among trees, but we thought there must be a road beyond it, so we climbed a sort of mound thing at the bottom of the field to see where the road was. The mound was all grown over with whippy little bushes that were budding big pale buds and there were little trampled paths leading in and out all over. I remember thinking that it looked a good place to play in. Children obviously played here. Then we got to the top of the hill and we could see the children.

They were in the garden of the big house. It was a boring red brick house that looked as if it might be a school. The garden, which we could look down into across a wall, was a boring school-type garden, too, just grass and round beds with evergreens in them. The children were all playing in it, very quietly and sedately. It was unnatural. I mean, how can forty kids make almost no noise at all? The ones who were playing never shouted once. Most of them were just walking about, in rows of four or five. If they were girls, they walked arm in arm. The boys just strolled in a line. And they all looked alike. They weren't alike. All the girls had different little plaid dresses on, and all the boys had different colored sweaters. Some had fair hair, some brown hair, and four or five of the kids were black. Their faces weren't the same. But they *were*, if you see what I mean. They all moved the same way and had the same expressions on their different faces. We stared. We were both amazed.

"They're clones," said Chris. "They have to be."

"But wouldn't clones be like twins?" I said.

"They're part of a secret experiment to make clones look different," Chris said. "They've managed to make their bodies not look alike, but their minds are still the same. You can see they are."

It was one of those jokes you almost mean. I wished Chris hadn't said it. I didn't think the children would hear me from where we were, but a man came up beside me from the bushes while Chris was talking, and I knew the man could hear. Luckily at that moment, a lady dressed a bit like a nurse came out into the garden.

"Come along, children," she called. "It's getting cold and dark. Inside, all of you."

The lady was one of the Mrs. Urs. As the children all obediently walked toward her, I remembered she was Phyllis Forbes. I was going to tell Chris, but I looked at the man first because it was embarrassing with him standing there. He seemed to have gone. So I looked at Chris to tell him, and Chris's face was a white staring blur, gazing at me.

"You look as if you've seen a ghost!" I said.

"I have," he said. "The ghost from my room. He was standing right beside you a second ago."

I ran then. I couldn't seem to stop myself. I went tearing my way through the bushes all across and down the little hill and then out into a field of some kind and then into another field after that. I remember a wire fence twanging and a hedge which scraped me all over, and a huge black and white beast suddenly looming at me out of the twilight. It was a cow, I think. I did a mad sideways swerve round it and ran on. I wanted to scream, but I was so frightened that all I could make was a little whimpering sound. After a while I could hear Chris pelting after me, calling out, "Cool it, Mig! Wait! He's not frightening at all, really!" I wanted to shout back "Then why did you look so scared?" but I could still only make that stupid mewing noise. "Hm-hm-hm!" I said to Chris, and rushed on. I don't know where all I went, with Chris rushing after me telling me to stop. It was getting darker all the time. But I think some of where I ran must have been the vegetable plots along the back of Cranbury, because it was all cold and cloggy and I kept treading on big clammy plants that went *crunch* and gave out a fierce smell of cabbage. My feet got heavier and heavier like they do in nightmares. I could see town lights twinkling to one side and orange streetlight shining steadily ahead, and I raced for the orange light with my huge heavy feet, and my chest hurt and I kept going, "Hm-hm-hm!" until Chris caught me up and I suddenly ran out of breath.

"Honestly!" he said. He was disgusted.

We were beside an iron fence just outside the station car park, with dew hanging off it and glittering on all the cars in the orange light. A train was just coming rattling into the station. I had a stitch in my side and I could hardly breathe. I lifted first one foot then the other into the light. They were both giant-sized with earth and smelled of cabbage. We looked at them and we laughed. Chris leaned on the fence and squealed with laughter. I hiccuped and panted and my eyes watered.

"It wasn't really the ghost," I said when I could speak. "Was it?"

"I just said it to frighten you," said Chris. "The result was spectacular. Get some of that mud off. Aunt Maria will be telling everyone we're drowned and Elaine will be giving Mum hell for letting Auntie get so worried."

Now I'm writing it down, I can see Chris was lying to make me feel better. I didn't realize then, and I did feel better. I stood on one leg and took my shoes off in turn and scraped them on the iron fence. Chris scraped his a bit, but he wasn't anything like as muddy. He had looked where he was going.

While we were doing it, the train had stopped and all the people from it began to come out of the station. They came one after another along past the fence under the light. They didn't look at us. They were all staring straight ahead and walking in the same brisk way, looking kind of dull and tired. "Rush-hour crowd," Chris said. "Funny to have it out here, too. I wonder where they all commute to."

"They look like zombies," I said. Most of them were

men and they mostly wore city suits. About half the line marched out through the gate at the end of the car park. We could hear their feet marching *twunka twunka twunka* down the road into Cranbury. The other half, in the same unseeing way, walked to cars in the car park. The space was suddenly full of headlights coming on and starters whining. "Zombies tired after work," I said.

"All the husbands of the Mrs. Urs," said Chris. "The Mrs. Urs take their souls away and then send them out as zombies to earn money."

"But the Mr. Urs don't realize," I said. "They've all been zombies for years without anyone knowing." The cars were all zooming out of the car park by then, *crunchle crunchle* as they came past us on the gravel, flaring headlights over us. The zombies in each car looked straight ahead and didn't notice us staring over the fence. Car after car. It was giving me a mesmerized feeling, until one crunched by that was blue, with one headlight dimmer than the other and dents in well-known places. "Hey!" I cried out. I hung on to the fence so that my hands hurt. "Chris, that was—!"

"No, it wasn't," Chris said. He was hanging on the fence, too. "It had the wrong number. I thought it was our car, too, for a moment, but it wasn't, Mig. Truly."

You can rely on Chris where numbers are concerned. He's *always* right. "It was awfully like ours," I said.

"Creepily like," Chris agreed. "I really did wonder if

they'd dried it out and mended the door and sold it to someone—for a second, till I looked at the number plate. The number plate always goes with the car. It's a crime to change it—so it has to be a different car."

By the time all the cars had driven away, the porter in seaboots was padding about in front of the station, closing it for the night by the look of it. We climbed over the fence and trotted out through the car park gates.

"We'd better not tell Mum," I said.

"No," said Chris. "We can tell her we've seen clones and zombies, but not about the car."

In the end, we didn't tell Mum anything much. We were in trouble—both of us for being so late and me about the state my clothes were in. Aunt Maria was really put out about my clothes. "So thoughtless, dear. I can't take you to the meeting looking like that."

"I thought your meeting was this afternoon," Chris said.

Mum shushed him. She was in a frenzy. The Mrs. Urs had been there all afternoon having their Circle of Healing and wolfing cake, and now Aunt Maria had announced that there was a meeting at Cranbury Town Hall she had to go to at seven-thirty. That is the reason I have been able to write so much of this autobiography. I have been left behind in disgrace because I have got my only skirt torn and covered in mud. I like being in disgrace. There is still some cake left. Aunt Maria used her low sorrowing voice on me and then told Chris he had to go instead. Mum took one look at Chris's face and martyred herself again by saying she would go with Aunt Maria.

I can't think why Aunt Maria needs Mum. When zero hour approached, Elaine and her husband came round with the famous wheelchair. Mr. Elaine—who is called Larry—is smaller than Elaine and I think he was one of the line of zombies who got off the train. Anyway he has a pale, drained, zombie-ish look and does everything Elaine says. The two of them unfolded the vast, shiny wheelchair in the kitchen and heaved Aunt Maria into it. Chris had to go away and laugh. He says Aunt Maria looked like the Female Pope. At zero hour minus one, Aunt Maria had made Mum array her in a large purple coat, with most of a dead fox round her neck. The fox's head is very real, with red glass eyes, and it spoiled my supper, because Aunt Maria *had* supper in it in case they were late. And her hat, which is tall and thin with purple feathers. The wheelchair looked like a throne when she was in it. She kept snapping commands.

"Betty, my umbrella, don't forget my gloves. Larry, mind the rug in the hall. Be careful down the steps."

And Elaine always answered for Larry. "Don't worry. Larry's got it in hand. Larry can do your steps blindfold." Larry never said a thing. He looked at me and Chris as if he didn't like us. Then he and Mum and

Elaine took Aunt Maria bumping down the front steps and wheeled her off down the street like a small royal procession.

The meeting was about Cranbury Orphanage. It turns out that the house where we saw Mrs. Ur and the clones—and the ghost—is Cranbury Orphanage. How dull. It makes the whole day seem dull now, if they were only orphans, not experimental clones after all.

Mum thought the meeting was pretty dull, too. When I asked her about it just now, she said, "I don't know, cherub. I was asleep for most of it—but I *think* they were voting on whether or not to build an extension to the orphanage. I remember a dreary old buffer called Nathaniel Phelps was dead against it. He talked for ages, until Aunt Maria suddenly banged her umbrella on the floor and said of course they were going to build the poor orphans a new playroom. That seemed to settle it."

I think Aunt Maria is secretly Queen of Cranbury—not exactly Uncrowned Queen, more like Hatted Queen. I am glad I am not an orphan in that orphanage.

four

We are feeding the gray cat now. Something very odd has turned up because of that, and we have met Miss Phelps who said things. Chris says the ghost comes every night. But I'll tell it in order.

Ghost first. I ask Chris about him every morning. Chris laughs and says, "Poor old Abel Silver! I'm used to him by now." I said yesterday why didn't Chris sleep on the sofa downstairs instead? He was looking tired. I know how *I'd* feel if I was woken by a ghost every night. But Chris says he likes the ghost. "He just searches the shelves. He's not doing *me* any harm."

It was after that that the cat turned up at the window again. It came and put its silly flat gray face up against the glass and mewed desperately. Chris said it looked like a Pekinese. Aunt Maria was banging away upstairs, shouting that her toast was wrong, and Mum was flying through the room to see to it. But she stopped when she saw the cat.

"Poor thing!" she said. "Not a Pekinese, Chris. It reminds me of something . . . someone . . . that face . . ." There were more bangs and shouts from upstairs. Mum shouted, "Coming!" and she was just leaving when Chris put on an imitation of Aunt Maria.

"He's eating my birds!" Chris shouted. He jumped up and flailed his arms at the cat the way Aunt Maria does. The cat stared. It looked really hurt. Then it ran away.

Mum and I both said, "What did you do *that* for?" While I was making more toast for Aunt Maria, Chris said he was sorry, he couldn't resist, somehow. The cat sort of asked for it. I know what he means. But Mum got really indignant.

She went looking for the cat after we'd got Aunt Maria dressed—which takes ages now, because Mum keeps trying to make Aunt Maria do something for herself. She says, "*Your* hands aren't the *least* arthritic, Auntie. Try doing up these hooks." Aunt Maria pretends to fumble for a bit and then says in a low sighing voice, "I'm old." Mum says, "Yes, but marvelous for your age!" in a special cheerful voice. Aunt Maria beams, "Thank you, dear. How kind! What a *devoted* nurse you are!" And I end up doing the hooks, or whatever, or she wouldn't be dressed by evening.

That day was fine. The sun came sideways across the

garden and seemed to bring green in among the brown of it for a change. Mum put her radio on the table beside Aunt Maria's roped-up sofa and firmly put the *Telegraph* on Aunt Maria's lap and told her we were all going to be busy in the garden.

Aunt Maria of course said, "I have so few people to talk to, dear!" and Chris of course muttered, "Yes, only thirteen Mrs. Urs," but Mum tore them apart and bundled us into the garden. I really thought the worm had turned and Mum had had enough of being martyred. But Mum never lies. She had me and Chris hanging up washing like mad in no time—all the clothes we'd got muddy in the dark and a whole row of Aunt Maria's sky-blue, baggy knickers that Chris calls "Auntie's Baghdads."

While we did that, Mum said, "Now I'm going to find that cat. It didn't go far."

She did find it, too. She called to us gently from the shed at the back behind the gooseberry bushes. Chris and I were doing an Arabic dance at the time, with the washing bowl and a pair of Baghdads. Chris still had the Baghdads on his head when we went over. He saw the gooseberry bushes and said, "*That's* where the orphans are cloned from!" The ghost and Aunt Maria between them have a bad effect on Chris. He's never sane now unless he's out in the town.

"Hush!" Mum said, and stood up holding the gray fluffy cat. "Chris, you look an utter ass! This poor beast is starving. She's skin and bone under this fluff!"

"She?" I said.

"Yes, it's a female," Mum said, and she tipped the cat upside down in her arms to show us. That cat is *soppy*. She lets you do anything with her. She lay on her back in Mum's arms, bending her front paws about and purring like a heavy motorbike. The only things she doesn't like are Aunt Maria and Elaine. Elaine put her head over the garden wall at that moment. That cat heaved out of Mum's arms and hid in the gooseberry bushes. Elaine didn't see it. She was staring at Chris with a pair of the Baghdads on his head, uttering her most clock-striking laugh.

"Good Lord, my lad!" she said. "You look like a ghostly court jester!" Chris went a little pale at that and stared, rather. But Elaine looked at Mum then. "You shouldn't do any washing," she said. "I *told* you to give it to me."

"Oh, *that's* all right," Mum said. "Mig got herself so muddy it had to be done by hand." Meaning, she is not going to let Elaine do her any favors.

"Be sure you give me the next lot then," Elaine commanded. Two-line smile, meaning This Is an Order. "I'm coming in this afternoon to sit with her while you're out."

"Oh? Am I going out?" Mum asked sweetly.

"You've got to buy Naomi more clothes," Elaine said,

and bobbed out of sight behind the wall.

"So I have!" murmured Mum. "Mig, how would you like a sack with holes in it?"

"She could manage with that hall rug," Chris said, "that we have to roll up every night."

"Yes, if I cut a hole in it for my head," I said.

Mum bent down and held out her arms coaxingly to the cat. "Disobey Elaine!" she said. "Good heavens! She'd beat us insensible with her torch. Or if we *really* annoyed her, she might even set Larry onto us." I've never heard Mum be so catty, not ever!

Talking of cats, the cat came leaping into Mum's arms, and it *was* starving. It ate two raw hamburgers and drank a bowl of milk in three minutes flat. The first thing Mum did when we were out that afternoon was to buy a whole cardboard box full of cat food. She's talking of taking the cat back to London with us. She says it's so affectionate. She keeps saying, "I can't *think* how it comes to be a stray! I thought gray Persians were rather valuable." She also sits it on the drain board and spends long ages rubbing the sides of its flat whiskery face. "Kutchi-wutchi-wutchi," she murmurs, staring deep into its glassy yellow eyes. "You *do* remind me of someone, but I can't think who!"

It's a terribly boring cat. About as interesting as a floppy cushion. But Chris and I look after it almost as eagerly as Mum does. We all know we're defying Elaine and Aunt Maria.

But of course we obeyed Elaine by going shopping for a new skirt for me. I wish Mum had defied Aunt Maria and let Chris come, too. But Aunt Maria did her soulful low booming voice and said, "My friends love to see young people," so Chris had to stay and help Elaine cut sandwiches. His face looked as if he was imagining cutting bread as sawing slowly through one of Aunt Maria's legs.

It was still beautifully sunny, with almost no wind. The sea was blue-gray and the tide was out. You'd have thought there would be somebody down on the sand at least, but Cranbury was like a ghost town. Not a soul was about.

"Perhaps it's early-closing day," Mum said.

But it wasn't. The shops were open. Mum went sailing down the street with her load of cat food, talking in her merriest, most ringing way. "What an odd place this is," she said. "There don't seem to be any children." The lace curtains all along the street jerked. I thought, except the clones, and walked a long way behind trying to look as if I didn't belong to Mum. When she's in that kind of mood she can be worse than Chris. It was Elaine's fault she was.

Sure enough, Mum fell into a long conversation in the clothes shop with the lady there, all about how quiet

Cranbury was. I could see the lady was embarrassed from the awkward way she said, "Well, there's a lot of retired people live here, you know."

"And no children at all?" Mum said. "There *must* be. You sell children's clothes."

"We don't get much call for them," the lady admitted, "except from tourists like yourself."

Then Mum explained at great embarrassing length that we were staying with Aunt Maria. I wish she wouldn't. I do think people ought to be more mysterious about themselves. And the lady got eager and sympathetic and kept saying, "Difficult to live with, is she?" in a way that was obviously fishing. So then Mum told her about the time when Aunt Marion was alive, and not on speaking terms with Aunt Maria. They both insisted we should see them, but they would not admit the other one existed. So that whenever we visited Cranbury we had to have tea twice, once with Aunt Marion and once with Aunt Maria. I remember it hideously. I was always sick on the way home.

The lady laughed and said, "Yes, she's always been like that. Miss Phelps is the latest. I feel sorry for Miss Phelps. Your auntie's friend Elaine used to do a lot for Miss Phelps—take her out in a wheelchair and so on—but since Miss Phelps and your auntie had words, I heard Mrs. Blackwell's been under orders not to do anything for her anymore."

Then Mum got an attack of crusading zeal and asked the lady ringingly if Miss Phelps would appreciate a visit from *us*. And the lady said, "Yes. Number twelve, she is, just across the road from you." Really, it is difficult having a martyred crusading saint for a mother sometimes. She forgot my skirt and had to go back for it. She only remembered when we'd walked right to the other end of town. Mum said it was such a fine day that she would let Elaine get on with the Mrs. Urs and get a bit of fresh air for a change. So we humped the cat food along the seafront, until we came to the concrete slope with the little boats pulled up on it. That was the first time we saw anyone. There were four or five men in big boots pottering about the boats.

"Ah! A rare sighting of the endangered human species," Mum said, and called out, "Good afternoon!" very loudly. Only two of the men looked up and only one nodded. "What a hole this is!" Mum said. I saw her notice the cliff under Cranbury Head and look away quickly. "I never did find out what caused the row between Aunt Marion and Aunt Maria," she said, with dreadful merriness. "I wonder what Miss Phelps said to her." Then she remembered my skirt. First she said I could run and get it. Then she saw my face and relented. "I left it," she said. "I'll go back for it. You take the cat food and wait in the main square. I seem to remember this picturesque little dump has a café there. I'll buy you an ice cream before we go back to the workhouse."

Which shows that Mum is a fairly human saint. But cat food weighs a ton. When I got to the main square I put it on the steps of the war memorial and wandered about. The café was shut. Of course. So I went down the street Mum was most likely to come to the square by so that I could wave and save her the journey when I saw her. And instead I saw a car parked by the drugstore. It was a blue car with well-known dents—the one we saw at the station the other night. It looked so like our old car that my heart began to bump and hammer in my throat, even though I could see its number plate. Ours had been a Y-registration. This was an H, and its number plate was all old and rusty. But it was the same kind of Ford, the same color exactly. I found myself thinking, I'll just go round on to the pavement and see if the dents in the driver's door are there. Dad had kicked it furiously the first time it stopped unlocking. And before I'd finished thinking that, I was round on the pavement, staring.

That door was quite smooth. It looked a slightly different color from the rest of the body. Its window was wound down and there was a blond lady sitting in the driver's seat busy doing her face in one of those little handbag mirrors. I hadn't seen her from behind because the car had high backs to the seats, like gravestones—just like ours again. She had a pouting mouth and cared-for dyed hair. In fact, she looked so exactly like I always imagined Verena Bland that Dad went away with, that the most awful suspicions went through my mind. My heart hammered even harder, and I went nearer—or I tried to. But I found I was sort of bending down, with a hand on each knee, in a most peculiar way. If you walk like that it's even more peculiar. And I thought of spies using handbag mirrors and car mirrors to watch people in. I thought, She's watching me in that mirror!

After that I was so terrified that she'd suspect my suspicions that I was forced to straighten up. I walked right up to the car window and I said, "Excuse me, miss."

I tried to get a sniff of the inside of the car as I said it, to see if it smelled of seawater or the same old smell as always, but all I got was an absolute blast of the blond lady's perfume. She turned her head with a jump. "Yes?" she said, surprised and unfriendly.

I hadn't a clue what I was going to say but somehow I found myself asking, ever so shy and pretty, "Excuse me, did you get your beautiful perfume at this drugstore here, miss?" I didn't know I had that much presence of mind.

She gave a sunny smile and shook her head. "No. It came from Bond Street in London. It's ever so expensive. You couldn't afford it, dear."

"I come from London," I said. "Do you live here, miss?" I was practically lisping. She must have thought

I had no brain at all. "You're ever so pretty. What's your name?"

She liked me thinking she was pretty. She gave a pleased wriggle and quite a sweet smile. "My name's Zenobia Bailey," she said. "I live here and I have to go home now." And she started the car and drove it away down the street.

I started to give her a sickly little good-bye wave, then gave it up. It had gone boring again, like the orphanage. It wasn't our car. She wasn't Verena Bland. And Mum was pounding up from the other direction with the cat food and the new skirt, saying, "Mig, for goodness' *sake*! Don't just go away and leave things like that! What were you doing?"

"Being a moron," I said. And I *still* think it *was* our car. I can't seem to shake myself out of it. Chris says that if it was—and he thinks it isn't—there are perfectly reasonable explanations. The insurance wrote it off and sold it, and the scrap yard found it worked and mended it and then sold it to Zenobia. Then why did they change the number plates? Because it isn't our car? Oh, I give up.

Chris is in a bad mood, anyway. It was a mistake to leave him with Aunt Maria and the Mrs. Urs. He said Something Awful again. Nobody would say what, though. Aunt Maria would only keep saying, "I'm so hurt and ashamed. But I forgive him of course." Then she says gently, "I shall pray for you, Christopher." It's a wonderful way to annoy Chris. He hates being given the wrong name, but he hates even more having to say his name is really Christian. If he tries, he has to shout, "CHRISTIAN!" at the top of his voice because Aunt Maria goes deaf on the spot.

Mum said Chris had been punished enough and, late at night, she got it out of Chris what he had done. It seems that mad Zoe Green had been one of the people who came for tea. All the other people there whispered warningly to Chris that he was to be nice to Zoe Green because of her son. "All I did," Chris said innocently, "was ask what was wrong with her son."

"Oh, did you?" said Mum. "I know you, Chris. I can just hear you doing it. 'But what's *wrong* with her son? Is he dead? Is he in prison for murder? Is he a sex maniac?' Louder and louder, until they could probably hear you at the town hall. I can see the look on your face while you did it, too. Don't do it again."

Mum was right. Chris went red and muttered, "Well, it had to be something like that, or she wouldn't have gone dotty, would she?"

Since then, Mum has kept announcing that Chris needs fresh air. She sends him out in the morning whenever she sees him alone in the room with Aunt Maria. She sends him out in the afternoon as soon as the Mrs. Urs start arriving. Chris doesn't mind. But I do. I have to be "dear little Naomi" and listen to the Mrs. Urs telling me how much Chris is upsetting Aunt Maria. "You know how sensitive she is," they say. "The least thing makes her so ill." Except for Elaine. Elaine just said bluntly, "I told you to stop that brother of yours. You'd better try."

I tried to defend Chris by saying he didn't understand old ladies.

Elaine fixed me with her fanatical eyes and grimmest look. "Oh, yes, he does understand," she said. "He knows just what he's doing. And it won't work. Not here. Not now." Then she added, over the shoulder of her black mac as she marched out, "It's a pity. I like him, you know."

The funny thing is that what Elaine said is true. I think she does like Chris, and I think Chris is up to something. I am the one who doesn't understand. I realized this when we went to see Miss Phelps this morning. I went with Chris because Mum had got sick of me complaining that Chris got all the fun.

"It won't be fun," Mum said. "She's a poor old lady and I want you to find out if there's anything we can do for her. You can try and stop Chris being rude, too, if you can—though I know that's the same as asking you to keep the sea back with a broom."

So we crossed the street to number twelve, Chris and me. Its lace curtains twitched like lace curtains in a panic when we knocked at the door. We stood there so long that we thought no one was going to open the door at first. When Miss Phelps did open it, we both stared.

"Oh, good morning. Chris and Mig, I believe," she said. She looks just like a gnome. She is tiny, much smaller than me, and she has a hump. Her eyes sort of slant in her withered face—and the glasses she wears sort of slant with her eyes. You can see she can hardly walk. She holds on to things and shuffles. But there is nothing wrong with her mind. She is brisk and direct and—well, the best way to put it is that she is interested in things and people for their own sakes. She does not want to make anyone do anything. You can't imagine how restful that is after Aunt Maria.

Somehow all that came over just from the way she said, "Good morning." Chris stopped looking long-suffering and gazed down at her with the same interest she was using on us. "Mum sent us over to see if there was anything you needed," he said.

"How kind of her," said Miss Phelps. "No. I can't say I have any crying need—except perhaps for better legs. But won't you come in? Word gets round in a place like Cranbury, you know, and I've heard a lot about you."

We went in, feeling a bit shy, into a long hall. There was an extraordinary noise coming from somewhere. It went *thump, bump* and then a desperate voice cried out, "Aa-aah!" as if someone was being killed. It startled me a lot until I remembered there were such things as television sets. I've been such days without a telly now that I've forgotten the sort of noises they make. I thought, Oh, good! We've come into a normal home!

"Go down the passage, then through the door on the right," Miss Phelps said. She shuffled after us, explaining, "I go rather slowly because I have a way of falling over. The doctor can't understand it. He calls it The Plunge."

It was a very ordinary room, with a plain sofa and a special high chair near the window with a table across it. We sat down on the sofa, facing the telly. The telly was off. Funny, I thought. Miss Phelps shuffled to the high chair and nipped up into it like a monkey or a small child. She has a perfect view of the street from there. She must watch us go in and out all day, perched in her chair like a gnome.

"No, I read a lot, too," she said, knowing what I was thinking. "I generally keep out of my neighbors' business, and out of quarrels, too, if I can. I like to stand aside."

"But you said something to Aunt Maria," Chris said.

Miss Phelps chuckled. "Yes, didn't I just!" she said. "But it was a perfectly objective general remark which I don't intend to repeat to you two. It was after she got rid of poor Lavinia."

"Lavinia's gone to her mother . . . hasn't she?" I said.

"Wherever it is, I think you'll find she's gone for good," Miss Phelps said. "Now what do you both think of Cranbury?" She made us talk about Cranbury for quite a while. We didn't say what we really felt, exactly, and Chris was surprisingly polite, but she knew what we meant.

"In other words, it's a hole," she said. "It's a very healthy hole, you know. People live to a surprising age here, but there isn't much to offer children out of season, I do agree."

Chris seemed to have been waiting for her to say something like this. He said, "What happened to Zoe Green's son?"

Miss Phelps turned in her high chair and looked at me. Then she turned herself to look at Chris. "You won't find that anybody speaks about him," she said. "Now I think I shall make you talk about London."

Chris said, "But I want to know. How long ago was it—whatever it was?"

"That I can't tell you," said Miss Phelps. "And I do like to hear about London, you know. As I said, few people talk about Antony Green. In fact, almost the only person who does is my brother. You'll want to speak to my brother, I suppose?"

"Yes, please," said Chris. "Where . . . ?"

"Come this way then." Miss Phelps climbed down from her chair and shuffled to the door. She opened it and shuffled across the hall, where she opened another door, while we both stood towering over her wondering what was inside. She turned round. "Do go in," she said, and she stretched her arm out to usher us in. At least, I think that was what she meant to do. But her arm seemed to take the rest of her with it. As we went into the room and found it almost bare, except for a man in a dressing gown standing like a statue and holding a sword pointing toward us across the top of his own head, Miss Phelps's gnomelike body swooped through the air in a graceful curve. Then she fell with a crash on the bare floor. It looked almost as if she had forgotten how to fly.

Chris and I both said, "Oh, dear!" and "Are you all right, Miss Phelps?"

The man with the sword never moved. He said irritably, "Not again, Amaryllis!"

"Yes. It's The Plunge today," Miss Phelps said, a bit breathlessly. She didn't try to get up. She just lay on the floor and said politely, "My brother Nathaniel. Christian and Margaret Laker, Nathaniel."

We stared from Miss Phelps on the floor to Mr. Phelps with his sword. He was the man who said, "Good afternoon," on the seafront the day Chris told me about the ghost. He has white hair and a white mustache and a thin, angry face. He said, "The art of swordsmanship, properly practiced, entails my standing here for another minute."

"By which time any self-respecting enemy will have stabbed you in the stomach," Miss Phelps observed, still lying on the floor.

"Oh, pick her up, can't you!" Mr. Phelps said angrily.

We got down and sort of crawled round Miss Phelps. But she said, very politely, "No, thank you. I think I shall lie here until I notice what I've broken this time."

So we got up again, feeling very silly. I stared at Mr. Phelps's long mauve ankles under his dressing gown and then at his sword. Chris sort of cleared his throat. Mr. Phelps said, "What in the world do you mean, bringing me two of the enemy?"

"They aren't the enemy," Miss Phelps said, lying there. "I checked."

"They're from number thirteen," said Mr. Phelps. He bared his teeth and stared up at his sword.

"We hate Aunt Maria as much as you do," I said.

"I doubt it," said Miss Phelps from beside my feet.

"I want to know about Antony Green," Chris said.

"What about him?" said Mr. Phelps. He lowered the sword at last, very slowly, and stood looking along it as if he thought it might have got bent.

"How long ago?" Chris said. "And—what happened?"

"How long?" asked Mr. Phelps, frowning at his sword. "Twenty years, I think. That's all I'm prepared to say until I know your motives, young man." He began making lunges with the sword, stamping with his slippers on the floorboards and going, "Aa-aah," when he stamped. That was the noise I thought was the telly. It must have been very uncomfortable for Miss Phelps on the floor.

Chris edged round past Miss Phelps's little goblin body until he was dangerously in the way of the sword, where he tried to catch Mr. Phelps's frowning eye. "There's a ghost in my room, sir," he said.

Mr. Phelps stopped with one foot about to stamp. He lowered his sword and his slipper and stared at Chris. "Why didn't you say so before, boy?" he said. Then he suddenly rounded on me. "Get her up, get her out of it," he said, pointing at Miss Phelps with his sword. "All women out of here."

Miss Phelps said, "I think I'm ready to stand up now." I bent down and heaved at her. She was so light. She came up as if she was floating, and she was so dignified that I had to let go of her as soon as her feet were on the floor. "Thank you," she said, shuffling into the hall. Then when we got to the other room, she said, "Do you know, that was a good fall! Nothing broke this time." Then she sat in her chair and made me tell her all about London for nearly half an hour, until Chris had finished talking to Mr. Phelps.

Elaine was right. Chris came out looking pretty thoughtful, and he wouldn't tell me what Mr. Phelps said. "Not your business, Mig," he said.

"Not in front of women and children, you mean!" I said crossly.

"That's roughly it," Chris said.

Sometimes I think everyone in Cranbury is mad, even me.

Five

It got madder yet. Perhaps Aunt Maria is the Hatted Queen of Cranbury because she's Queen of Mad Hatters. She knew at once that we had been to see Miss Phelps. "Such a quaint little thing, isn't she?" she said. "I always try to be kind to her, but she makes it so difficult. I expect you found her very hard to talk to." Aunt Maria looked down at her lap, the way she always does when she thinks she is forced to say something terrible, and added, "So uncharitable!"

Chris gave me an explosive look. I said Miss Phelps had fallen over.

"Poor thing!" Aunt Maria said. That was her special sincere voice. "That will teach her to make rude remarks. Well, you won't be going *there* again, so that's all right."

Elaine came marching in to tell us the same thing after lunch, when Chris and I were washing up. "You two," she said. "Cut the Phelps connection—understand? We don't have anything to do with number twelve." And before Chris could think of a rude remark, Elaine went off up the garden, where Mum was petting the cat and pretending to garden. The cat hid, and Elaine strode around forbidding Mum to let us go near Miss Phelps. Then telling Mum she had done a good job on the roses but she ought to tackle some more of the weeds before they started growing—on and on, until I wondered why Mum didn't hit her. Chris says he wouldn't dare hit Elaine, either. She's so tall and wiry. But I saw Mum go for Dad several times when Dad was trying to hit Chris or me. Mum's brave enough. But she's just too civilized to hit Elaine.

This is what puts Mum at a disadvantage. Aunt Maria and Elaine—and some of the Mrs. Urs—can *rely* on Mum being too civilized to fight back. What's the good of being civilized, that's what I want to know? It just means other people can break the rules and you can't.

Anyway, *I* tried to break the rules when all the Mrs. Urs came to tea. It's not as easy as you'd think. There were seven of them, so there was a crowd in the dining room and not enough cake for me. Chris had taken a huge slice in his pocket when Mum booted him out. I was squashed between Hester Bailey and Phyllis Forbes, but that didn't stop the other five leaning over and telling me:

1. "Naomi, dear, we don't like to think of you under bad influence."

2. "Naomi, dear, I heard something about you I hope isn't true."
3. "Naomi, dear, don't worry your aunt this way."
4. "Naomi, dear, I was so sad to hear you saw Miss Phelps."
5. "Naomi, dear, Miss Phelps isn't a *nice* person to know."
6. This was Phyllis Forbes: "She's all right, but her *brother*!"

First I tried saying in a loud voice, like Chris had, "What's *wrong* with Miss Phelps?" And only Aunt Maria seemed to hear at all.

"What's wrong with home helps?" says Aunt Maria. "*Dear* Lavinia! I hadn't a word to say against Lavinia. Devoted."

So then I pulled Phyllis Forbes's sleeve and asked how the orphans were getting on. I said, "Those dear little children you look after . . . "

She just turned away. She never talks about the clones. That's why I asked.

So that left Hester Bailey. Sensible, ordinary-looking Hester Bailey who gave me those pictures. I said, "Do you have a daughter called Zenobia, Mrs. Bailey?"

"Yes, as a matter of fact I do," she said in her sensible way. Then, just as I began to feel interested, Hester Bailey held her hand out to show someone about two feet high. "About this tall," she said. "A sweet child, vibrant with imagination. What a pity," she said, giving me one of her most sensible smiles, "that such a daughter only exists in my imagination."

"Well," I said. "I suppose an imaginary daughter's better than none."

"I do agree," she said. I think she's even madder than Zoe Green.

And Mum seems to have caught it now. She smuggled the gray cat up to our bedroom. It wasn't hard to do. For one thing, the cat seemed to be expecting it. When I opened the front door to put the milk bottles out, the cat was sitting on the doorstep like a hassock escaped from church. It simply strolled indoors, tail up, cool as if it owned the place. Mum called to Chris to put the electricity off, snatched the cat up, and raced upstairs so fast that her candle went out.

She was feverishly fumbling about trying to light the candle again when I came in with my candle. "Oh, good! Light!" she said. She snatched my candle and nearly put that out, too, lighting hers with it. Then she rushed to the shelf and took down Lavinia's silver-framed photo of Lavinia and her mother. "That's it!" Mum cried, and shoved candle and photo toward me. "Don't you think she's the spitting image of Lavinia?" she cried.

"Lavinia's mum?" I said. "Yes, I told you. Twins."

"No, no!" cried Mum. "The *cat,* Mig!"

Naturally, Aunt Maria woke up and shouted, "Is there a bat? Has a bat got in the house?"

I looked at the cat. It was lying on my pillow looking even more than usually like a floppy cushion. It looked calmly back at me.

"It's all right, Auntie!" Mum called. "I just said I was getting *fat*!" And in a whisper to me, "*Isn't* it like her?"

"Yes, you'll need a hat for church tomorrow, dear!" called Aunt Maria.

"And a sprat on a mat where I spat," says Chris on the stairs, listening in.

"What's *that*?" yells Aunt Maria.

By this time I'd got the giggles, and Mum was looking tragic and misused. I said hurriedly that the cat was probably exactly like Lavinia. Mum relaxed. Chris went to bed and Aunt Maria went back to sleep. "Why are you so worked up about what the cat looks like?" I said.

Mum was in bed and so was the cat by then. We shall have to buy some flea powder. "Because I think it may be Lavinia's cat," Mum said. "I think she may have left it behind expecting Aunt Maria would feed it . . . or she may have owned it secretly . . . or, oh, all sorts of things."

"How do you work *that* out?" I said.

"Because animals do grow to look like their owners," Mum said seriously. "Everyone knows that."

I would have hooted with laughter, only I knew it

would wake Aunt Maria again. So I just got on with writing this. And while I did, it dawned on me that I am just as crazy as Mum. I am being quite as unreasonable over that blue Ford which is so like our old car.

Since then, the cat gets called Lavinia. The name seems to suit her. She answers to it quite well, and she seems to have got more interesting with a name, somehow.

But something really *extraordinary* has just happened. Can a cat be that intelligent? It's hard to believe. Anyway, I wrote quite a lot of this the next morning. It is Sunday. Aunt Maria has gone to church in her dead fox and her high hat and her wheelchair, in one procession of Elaine, Mum, and voiceless Larry as before. She wanted us, too, but Mum said we hadn't got proper clothes. Talking of clothes, Elaine has a black coat on today which is quite a clever imitation of the usual mac, and a black beret. All she needs is jackboots and a rifle, though Chris says a stocking mask over her face would improve it. Chris has gone to the beach.

I had to stop writing and let Lavinia out. She was urgent. And I am scared of them coming back and finding a cat in the house. But Lavinia wouldn't go out unless I came into the garden, too. I kept opening the door, and she kept backing away from it, and looking at me and then mewing to go out when I shut the door—

cats can be maddening. So I stomped out, holding my pen and rather cross. And Lavinia ran away from me. It must have been because I was cross.

"Oh, God!" I said. "She thinks I'm like Elaine." I felt a beast. So I called and called, and she came out from the gooseberry bushes, just a little way. When I went to get her, she ran away again, into the garden shed. I went in there and looked. She was crouched up on a sloping high shelf full of flowerpots and cobwebs. "Do come down," I said. "I'm not like Elaine—really. I'm sorry." But she wouldn't come. She just crouched away backward when I tried to reach her. I had to get an old bucket and stand on it upside down before I was tall enough to grab her. "I don't know why I'm doing this," I told her as I grabbed. "Unless it will *prove* I like you or something."

She tried to get away when I thought I had her, and I unbalanced and tried to save myself on the shelf. And the whole shelf came down in a rain of flowerpots, dust, Lavinia, and garden catalogs covered with cobwebs. I stood in the ruins staring at a fat, faded exercise book that had been in the pile of catalogs. It was two shades paler and covered in those brown dots that grow on paper in garden sheds, but I knew what it was even before I'd got enough dust out of my eyes to read my own writing on the front.

"The Story of the Twin Princesses," by Naomi

Margaret Laker. That was my story that had still been hidden in our car when Dad drove off to France in it with Verena Bland. It had still been in the car when Dad stormed off after seeing us at Christmas, because I kept forgetting to ask for it what with all the quarreling there had been.

"So Dad *did* get here!" I said.

I looked for Lavinia then. She was sitting outside the door of the shed, giving herself a good, proper wash. It's the first time I've seen her wash. She looked very pleased with herself. She wouldn't come indoors when I went in with the exercise book. She seemed to know they'd be back from church soon.

I've looked at the book a hundred times since then. I've thought round and round. The book is very dusty and rather damp, but I *know* it has never been wet—not wet the way a book would have been which had been in a car that had fallen into the sea. The story I dropped in my bath dried all wavy, with brown marks, and the printed lines were washed out on some pages, as well as a lot of the writing. This book is flat and none of the ink has run. It doesn't even smell of sea, but it does, behind the dust, smell just faintly of the inside of our car. So what is it doing hidden in Aunt Maria's garden shed? Someone hid it, someone tall enough to reach that shelf, and I'd never have found it but for Lavinia.

That someone *has* to be Dad. I think he did get to

Aunt Maria's house after all, and he was coming away when he went off the cliff. But why didn't Aunt Maria *say* he came here? I know Mum would say the shock was too much for Aunt Maria and she forgot, or something. Or could Dad have sneaked into the house? I don't know. But my first thought was that Dad had left a message in the exercise book. I shook it in case there was a loose paper, but there wasn't. Then I went carefully through every page. Because it was such a nice fat book, I'd left every other page blank when I wrote that story, so that I could write notes and corrections on the empty page. It was a new, experimental method of writing that didn't seem to suit my genius. I got stuck in that story worse than I've ever been before. But it had left a lot of places where Dad could have written something if he'd wanted. And he hadn't. I even held each page up at eye level and looked across it, in case there were dents, like in detective stories, where something had been written in invisible ink. The trouble is, *I* had made dents writing deeply, thoughtfully, and stuckly, but I quite honestly can't find any dents that aren't obviously mine. So I am as puzzled as ever. I am hiding the book to show Chris.

I did show Chris but not till the middle of the night. Elaine was here all evening, with Larry Mr. Elaine. Larry actually spoke once or twice. He handed Aunt Maria official-looking letters and said, "This is from the tax office. This is from the broker," in a low, respectful voice. I think he is a lawyer. Elaine took her black coat off and hung it on a chair, but it didn't make much difference. She had a black dress underneath. She talked to Chris mostly, in a loud jolly voice, saying things like, "And what were you up to all day, my lad? I had news of you up on the Head and then over by the orphanage and off in Loup Woods, until I thought you must be in several places at once!"

This made Chris wriggle, rather, and grin, but he didn't seem annoyed. Mum started another sweater sleeve. I think she is knitting clothes for an octopus. I tried to draw a picture of Aunt Maria, but I couldn't show anyone because it went wrong and made her look like an insect. Mum saw it when we were getting ready for bed and Lavinia was sitting purring on my pillow again. We *must* get some flea powder.

"Oh, *Mig*!" Mum said reproachfully, holding my drawing under the candlelight. I felt bad. Aunt Maria had been like a teddy bear again when we put her to bed. "I know what you mean, though," Mum said. She smiled her bright and indulging smile. "She's a large, golden, furry insect. A queen bee. That's how all the Mrs. Urs think of her, I'm sure. It amuses me the way they all run around her and make sure she's happy, just as if they were workers and she were their queen. It's funny."

"If it makes you laugh," I said, and I pushed Lavinia

out of the way and pretended to go to sleep. I waited until Aunt Maria was snoring and Mum was almost snoring. Then I got up in the dark. I heard Lavinia thump down off the bed and come after me, but that didn't help. I was terrified. My hands were curled up and cold, but wet on the palms, and my heart was banging in my throat till it ached. Suppose I meet the ghost! I kept thinking. It was worse on the landing, where there was Aunt Maria's night-light shining round her bedroom door. There was just enough light to show me how pitch-dark it was. I nearly ran away from the big clock where I'd hidden the book. It looked like a person. *Clunk!* it went as I took the book out from behind it. I was so scared, I dived for the stairs.

"Is that you, Naomi?" called Aunt Maria. "What are you doing, dear?"

As I was halfway downstairs, I couldn't say I was going to the john. I said, "I'm hungry, Auntie. I'm going to look for a cookie."

"Be careful you don't fall, dear," called Aunt Maria.

I stood on the stairs waiting for her to start snoring again for about a year. Only Lavinia fluffily rubbing round my legs kept me sane—and even so I kept thinking, What if a light comes on and I find she's only a bundle of bones and cobwebs! But six months after I thought that, there came the well-known rasping snore from Aunt Maria. *Zzz zzz,* the queen bee buzzing, I thought, as I fled downstairs.

Chris's door was half open. There was a scrape and a flare inside the room as Chris lit his candle. "Come in and shut the door," he whispered. "What's up?" And when I'd shut the door, he said, "You sat there all evening looking like a rabbit in someone's headlights. I knew you'd come down. You should learn to hide your feelings a bit."

Ghost or not, the room Chris has is a nice room. It's cozy. The gold print on all the books glints by candlelight and the room smells of books. Chris has added improvements: a hanging flower basket over his bed that holds matches, cookies, and a book; an oil lamp; a fishing line hooked to the ceiling that is supposed to draw the curtains; and a thermometer propped on the bookshelf by the window.

"That's for the ghost," Chris explained. "They're supposed to make a cold spot where they appear, but I don't think this one does. Why did you bring that cat?"

"I didn't. She just came," I said. I showed him the book. "Know what this is?"

"'The Collected Works of N. M. Laker,'" Chris said. "You wrote it last year and got sick in the car—oh!" And he was impressed enough to light his oil lamp. "So Dad *did* get as far as this house," he said. "Give it here. Is there a message in it?"

But Chris couldn't find any message in the book,

either. I told him all about how I had found it trying to get Lavinia down and how it had to be a tall person like Dad who put it on the shelf.

"Elaine could have reached," said Chris.

"Yes, but *why*?" I said. "Why didn't Aunt Maria say Dad came here, if he did?"

"Guilt, I should think," said Chris.

"Guilt? Oh, you can't mean that!" I said. "Should we go to the police?"

Chris was looking through and through the book with my story on every other page. He said in a casual sort of way, "I haven't seen a single bobby in Cranbury, but I'm willing to bet he'll be a zombie like Larry when we do see him. Try if you like, Mig. But I'd rather you waited. This book means *something*, if I could just work it out. For one thing, how did the cat know it was there?"

"She couldn't have," I said. "She must have been living in the shed and I frightened her and she went back there."

Chris turned and looked at Lavinia. She looked back—she was sitting neat and upright in the exact middle of Chris's pillow, staring out of flat yellow eyes from her stupid flat gray face. Her tail was wrapped neatly in front of her stumpy front paws, which turn outward rather. "Like an old woman's feet," I said. "She's an old maid cat."

"I wonder!" said Chris. He made an incredulous

laugh. "I wonder, Mig! Mum could be right! Hadn't Lavinia got a wide flat sort of face and gray hair? I remember her turned-out feet. Her toes were humpy."

I was beginning to say that a joke was a joke, but no one can *really* turn a person into a cat, when I had a most peculiar feeling. Let's see if I can describe it. First, it was as if at the back of my mind somewhere I was out-of-doors. There was that open feeling you get. It was as chilly, wherever it was at the back of my mind, as those leaves I knelt on in the wood. With it I could sort of sense grass rustling, wind blowing, and the smell of earth, mixed with that almost gluey smell some new buds have. I had just noticed that, when the wind bringing the feeling seemed to be blowing on my back. I came up in goose pimples and smelled earth stronger than ever. The lamp and the candle both sort of faded, like when the moon goes behind a cloud. The cat jumped to all four feet and stood in an arch, glaring, twice the size with wildly standing hair.

"Is it the ghost?" I said.

"Yes—he's coming," said Chris. "Don't stay in here! Out, out, out!"

I don't remember getting up off Chris's bed. I was at the door and I dragged it open, and Lavinia nearly tripped me up in her hurry to get through it first. She fled upstairs into the dark, and I fled after her, and I wasn't scared of the dark a bit. I remember thinking how brave Chris was as I got myself into bed beside warm, warm Mum, and then I nearly jumped out again with a yell until I realized that Lavinia had got down into the bed, too. She stayed there, crouching by my feet, and no amount of shoving would make her budge. She was still there this morning.

"We *must* get some flea powder," Mum said. Chris came down to breakfast scratching, too. But he didn't look as tired as I did.

"Mig and I will go and get some flea powder," Chris said. He had thought of something he needed to tell me, I could see by his face. Mum saw, too, and told me to go.

"What's that, dear? I don't need knee powder," said Aunt Maria. "My knee only comes on in the winter."

"Sea chowder," said Chris.

Mum said very loudly and clearly, "Mig and Chris are going to buy some seafood for lunch, Auntie."

"Chris can go," said Aunt Maria. "I want my little Naomi by my side."

"Auntie," said Mum, "isn't it enough to have me tied to the house waiting on you hand and foot, without making a prisoner of Mig, too?" Now, the way she looked at Aunt Maria made us sure the worm had turned at last.

"I stand rebuked," said Aunt Maria, with a merry little laugh. "What a strict little nurse you are, Betty! Let them go and buy your face powder, dear. But you won't get whelks on a Monday."

Arguing with Aunt Maria is like that. You end up wondering what you were talking about. Chris and I laughed about it all the way to the seafront. We went to the sea because Chris said it was the most private place. It wasn't. Hester Bailey passed us, all wrapped up, with a little dog on a lead; then Benita Wallins stumping along with a plastic bag of shopping; then Phyllis and Selma Ur, and it was, "Goooood morning! Auntie well?" from each.

"There seems to be an alert out," Chris said. "I wonder if Aunt Maria knows what you found. Oh, Lord! Here comes Mr. Phelps now. Let's go down on the sand and wait for some peace."

Mad Mr. Phelps strode past us swinging his walking stick. "Morning, Christian," he said, taking no notice of me.

"Morning," Chris said, rather grudgingly over his shoulder, as he scrambled down on to the beach. The tide was out a long way. Chris ran toward the sea, floundering and crunching in the banks of pebbles, and then sprinting on the flat brown sand beyond, setting spurts of water flying. When I caught him up, he was sitting on a rock watching the waves roll seaweed about, panting. He was awfully pleased with himself. "Good," he said. "Phelps knows I found something at last."

"How does he?" I said. "Why should he? Besides, *I*

found my story, not you."

"Throw stones," said Chris. "Look casual. We mustn't look as if we're talking about anything important."

I threw stones. It was too cold in the wind not to keep moving about. But I was annoyed at Chris for being so pleased and mysterious. "Tell me," I said, "or I may throw stones at you."

"He says, 'Good morning,'" Chris said. "I say, 'Morning,' if I've got something. If I say, '*Good* morning,' it means I've got *it*. We arranged it the day Miss Phelps fell down."

"What's *it*?" I said. "What's it all about?"

"The thing the ghost is looking for, of course," said Chris. "He needs it. It contains most of Antony Green's power, and Mr. Phelps is the last one left now. He's got a right to it. He was Antony Green's second in command before they did for Antony Green."

"*Who* did for Antony Green?" I said.

"The same people who did for Dad. Obviously," Chris said. He began to ramble along the sand, throwing stones into the sea. The wind was nothing like as strong as it had been that first day, but it was still hard to hear him. I thought he said, "Mrs. Urs," as he went.

I ran after him. "Mr. Phelps is awfully mad," I said.

"I knew you wouldn't understand," Chris said. "Being female puts you automatically on the other side."

That really annoyed me. "No, it doesn't. I'm neutral

like Miss Phelps," I said. "And I want to know. Or are you being mysterious about nothing?"

We went rambling and wrangling along beside the waves until our feet were crusty with wet sand. Chris kept squirting out bits of explanation, the way he had talked about the ghost, in jerks. I think he was scared *and* ashamed of thinking some of the things he was thinking, too. He rather thought Mr. Phelps was mad. "He's a fitness freak," he said. "He does judo as well as that sword stuff. When he comes along the front, he's coming back from swimming. In all weathers. He says it's the way he stays above the common herd." Worse than Dad.

"Yes, but," I said, "what has my story in the garden shed to do with Mr. Phelps and Antony Green and the ghost?"

"It proves Dad did see Aunt Maria, probably. Right?" said Chris. "Now Dad is a native of Cranbury, remember. He'd know the whole story of Antony Green, and he'd know what the ghost was looking for. Suppose he came and stayed with Aunt Maria. Lavinia would be in the room you and Mum have, so Dad would have the room I'm in, wouldn't he?"

"So it *is* Dad's ghost!" I cried out.

"No, it isn't, you fool!" said Chris. And he went running away on top of his own reflection shining down in the wet sand. I couldn't make him stop for ages. But at last he stood still and said unfairly, "Have you calmed down? Right. Then suppose Dad saw the ghost and looked for what it was looking for and found it. What would he do then? It's valuable, remember, and he wouldn't want Aunt Maria to know he'd found it."

We stood facing one another on top of our reflections, with the wind clapping our anoraks. Chris looked deadly serious. It was the way Mr. Phelps looked holding his sword. *He's* mad now! I thought. I said, "He'd hide it in that place in the car where I put my story. But he had to take my story out to make room for it and hide that. Chris, what happened then?"

"Somebody found out," Chris said. He went running off again, calling over his shoulder, "Did our car fall off the cliff? Did it? Whee!"

I stood there. I thought, *I'm* mad, too. That blue car. I ran after Chris. "Chris! I met the car again outside the drugstore. Let's go and buy flea powder."

"Let's," said Chris. "I can pick the back lock. I got good at it."

But we didn't find the car, not outside the drugstore or anywhere else we looked. It's just dawned on me where we *should* have looked—in the station car park where we saw it first. We'd better look there tomorrow—though I still think everyone's mad.

SIX

We found the car. I don't know how to write about all this. It's so strange. I had to go upstairs and write it while Aunt Maria waits for the Mrs. Urs to come calling. Mum has gone out. She said it was only fair, after she let me and Chris go off two mornings running. So I have left Chris being talked to by Aunt Maria. It's quite a risk. I know he'll say something again. I'll go down and pretend to get out the cake when I hear the row start. But I just have to get this down.

The flea powder makes me sneeze, but it seems to have worked. Today Chris insisted he needed me to go out with him again. He had thought of the station car park, too.

Aunt Maria made her low reproachful noise. "I see so few people these days. Are you sure Naomi isn't avoiding me, Betty, dear?"

"Of course not," said Mum inventively. "I've asked Mig to choose me some new wool at the handicraft shop. I can't trust Chris with colors."

"Yes, that *is* woman's work," Aunt Maria agreed. "Dear little Naomi. A little woman."

So I had to tote a bag of pea green fluffy wool all round Chris's devious route to the station. First we went along the seafront. There was only Hester Bailey and dog today.

"Her small obnoxious cur," Chris called it. Because there was only Hester Bailey, he would have it that the Mrs. Urs had decided we didn't realize what finding my story meant. I still think that is imagination, about the Mrs. Urs, but I humored Chris. And then Mr. Phelps came striding toward us, tweaking his walking stick smartly and bending into the wind. Chris said, "*Good* morning."

Mr. Phelps almost missed his step. For a moment I thought he was going to fall over his stick. It faltered in midtweak. But he made it into a nod at me somehow, though he was staring into distance over my head. He has fanatical eyes, as bad as Elaine, the same gray as the sky is today, like two fanatical holes in his head. Then he strode on without a word.

"Chris!" I whispered. "We haven't found the car yet!"

"Yes, but I know it's there," Chris said. My private feeling suddenly was that the car was bound to be hidden in a locked garage somewhere, but I humored Chris again and we went round and round Cranbury until we got to the vegetable plots I had run through that day we saw the clones and the zombies. We got in by a stile and went up beside the hedge until we could see the roofs of the cars in the car park. Chris made us both sit down, out of sight from the station, to spy out the land. Of course we couldn't see anything from there. We had to get over the fence again and dodge about among the cars, bent over so that the porter in boots wouldn't see us. I felt very silly. I kept wondering why I was so nervous when we weren't doing anything wrong. I jumped when a pebble clanged off my foot onto a car, and expected the porter to come charging out shouting, "Hey, you!"

We never saw him. But we saw the car in the middle of the second row along, between two much shinier, newer ones. We sat down on the gravel beside it, out of sight, in a sort of canyon of car smelling of petrol and tire.

"It *is* ours, surely," whispered Chris. "That rusty place like a map of Australia."

"It's got a new door the other side," I whispered.

"Makes sense," Chris whispered. "It wouldn't unlock and Dad kicked it half to blazes. Come on. I'm going to get it open." He went crawling off to the back of it. I lugged the knitting wool after him and squatted watching while he dug away at the hatchback lock with his penknife. I think it was the tensest few minutes either of us had known. Chris was a strange patchy white color by the time the lock gave a tinny *sprung*! and he pulled up the hatch door. That whining sound, with a small *boing* from one side, was so familiar. I knew it was our car just from that noise. I think Chris did, too. He certainly knew the moment he looked inside. He was holding the door down so that it didn't bob up above the car roof, and his face suddenly flooded dark red. He said, "Oh, God. It is our car. That toffee's still stuck to the carpet." His voice was all on one note.

I looked in. My heart began hitting my throat when I saw the toffee. It had my teethmarks in it and it was all blue hairs from the trunk carpet. But it was the smell most of all. There was no sea smell and no rust smell. Just our dirty-old-car smell. I could tell Chris had come over queer because of that smell.

"It's all right," I said. "I'll get it."

I dumped the knitting wool beside the toffee and crawled in, over the backseat where Chris and I had fought since we were tiny, over the egg stain across the hump in the floor, to squeeze between the two gravestonelike front seats. There was Zenobia Bailey's perfume there on top of the car smell. I took deep breaths like somebody suffocating and reached in under the dashboard to the hiding place. The thing in there felt like a cigar box. By that time I felt as if I was running out of air. I just grabbed it and backed out in a rush.

"Put it in with the wool, and let's go!" Chris hissed at me.

So I jammed the box or whatever in the bag among the pea green wool and backed away. Chris put down the door with the firm thump that usually locked it again. Then we ran. Bent over and gasping, we ran and ran. It was like my mad rush after we saw the clones, only in the opposite direction and trying to hide all the time. I ran out of breath completely when we got to the cow field.

"Where are we going?" I said with what felt like my last gasp. We were behind a hawthorn bush covered with enough bright green buds to hide us.

"That—mound by the—orphanage," panted Chris. "Mr. Phelps is going to meet us there at twelve. He said—the time was important."

"Why *there*?" I said.

"Because of Antony Green," said Chris, and he set off running again.

It was only quarter to twelve when we got to the mound. We went up one of its little muddy paths and sat down to wait at the top. We were in the middle of a lot of these whippy bushes with big pale buds, hidden from the orphanage, where it was all quiet and windless, in a sort of chilly bush.

"Let's have a look at it," said Chris.

I took the thing out. It was a flattish box, but it wasn't

a cigar box. Whatever it was made of wasn't wood, or metal, and it was too warm to be plastic, though it sounded like plastic when I tapped it with my fingernail. Maybe it was bone. It was carved all over in patterns, swirly interlacing pictures that were colored in every shade of green you could ever imagine—gray green, faded yellow green, bright dragon green, all greens, right through to sad dark green that was nearly black. It was wonderful. We sat staring at it. It almost made sense, as if the green pictures were meant to tell you something. I almost knew what, too.

That was when the clones turned up. We looked up to find orphanage kids standing silently all around us, staring at the box as well.

"Pretty," said the one nearest, when she saw I had seen her.

They gave me quite a shock. They had come so quietly, and they looked so much alike, even close up, in spite of all being different colors and shapes of children, and they didn't move or jig about the way ordinary kids do. Chris muttered things angrily. I don't blame him. They were irritating, standing gooping like that.

"What are you going to do with it?" said another one.

"Give it to someone. Go away," said Chris.

They went on standing there.

"It's not interesting," said Chris.

That was a silly thing to say. That box was the most

interesting thing I'd ever seen. It was like something alive. It seemed to get more interesting the longer you looked. I was kind of bent over it, and the clones were all craned in different directions so that they could see it round me.

"Aren't you going to open it?" one of them asked.

As soon as he—or she—asked that, it was obvious we ought to open the box. I could see the catch on one side of the lid, a little clawed green clasp, and I pushed it up with my thumb. It moved easily. Chris said, "Mig, you're not to! Don't touch it!" But by that time my fingers were under the lid and the lid seemed to come up of its own accord.

I think the lid was even more beautifully green and complicated on the inside. But I didn't really notice, because whatever was inside the box started to come out at once. It wasn't quite invisible. You could tell it was bulging and billowing out of the box in clouds, fierce and determined and impatient. The clones all stepped back a solemn pace to give it room. It was all round me. The air felt thick, so that I had to press against it to move, even just to breathe, and it fizzed in a funny way in my hair and on my face. I didn't know what it was, but I could tell it was very forbidden.

Chris shouted out, "Oh, you stupid *girl*!" I had one hand under the box and the other against the lid, squeezing with all my might to try and shut it by then. But the stuff coming out held it open against me as hard as if the hinges were never made to bend. I knew it was horribly dangerous stuff—or perhaps, now I think, I knew it was a terrible waste to let it all out—and I pressed and pressed to get the box shut again. Chris scrambled over and put his hands over mine and we both pushed frantically. The lid didn't even start to give until the box was at least half empty. Then it went down, slowly, slowly, with more powerful stuff escaping the whole time. It must have taken us a good five minutes to get it shut again.

Meanwhile the stuff that was out was doing all sorts of strange things. You could tell it was there because it rippled everything it touched—not like hot air ripples things, but in a way that showed it was changing the substance of the bush or the person or the earth it passed through. Chris and I got rippled furiously. Some of the stuff spiraled hugely into the sky. I could see more eddying slowly down into the ground. But a lot of it lingered about, writhing the bushes, forming swirls and shapes as strange as the pictures on the box, and curlicues of nothing. Some of them were horrifying, and one clone who got in the midst of those covered her head in her arms and whimpered. A lot were splendid and solemn. The clones waved their arms at them in a stiff sort of way and looked wondering, and the curlicues of nothing climbed and twisted and wove around them until the stuff must have got thinned away by the air. Anyway, it went. One clone suddenly burst out laughing. A twist of nothing was hovering between his hands like a cross between a dust devil and an invisible bird. He was still holding it and laughing, and the rest of the stuff was fading into the earth in dying twirls, when Mr. Phelps came storming through the bushes slashing his stick.

He was furious. The orphans stared and then ran, just the way the cat runs away from Aunt Maria. But it was me Mr. Phelps went for, stick up ready to hit me. "You stupid little female!" he said. It was a low snapping snarl that was far more frightening than a shout. I dropped the box and put one arm up. "Half of it *gone*!" he said. "My last hope against this monstrous regiment of women, and it has to be a female who lets it out! You deserve to be whipped, girl. And you, boy, for letting her!"

I heard his stick swish. I think Chris got in the way. There was a thump and Chris said, "Don't *do* that! We were only trying to help!"

"Steal it, you mean, just as your father did!" snarled Mr. Phelps. "Get out. Get out of my sight. And don't let your sister near me again, or I won't be responsible for what I do!"

Chris and I pulled one another up, and we ran. Chris remembered the knitting wool, not me. I remember him humping it along, panting, "Oh, Lord, Mig, this is a mess! I thought he was the goodie and Aunt Maria was the baddie, but I'm not sure now. I *wish* you hadn't opened that box!"

I wished I hadn't, too, so I didn't answer.

And I wish it even more now. I don't know what to do. Cranbury isn't just mad. It's a nightmare.

I finished my writing. I went downstairs. I think I must have gone rather quietly because I was still thinking about that amazing box. Chris and Aunt Maria didn't hear me. As I came down she was saying, "Snoring, dear? I wasn't snoring. I'm awake. I've been talking to you."

"Boring," Chris said. "B—O—R—I—N—G, that's what I said you were."

I thought, Oh, dear! and hurried. Aunt Maria said, more in sorrow than anger, "You poor boy. I shall pray for you, Christopher."

"And get my name right!" Chris snarled. "It's *Christian*, you murderess!"

Aunt Maria said, "*What!*" in a little faint voice. I felt weak and sort of sinking and had to prop myself up in the doorway. I said, "Shut up, Chris." I think I did, but neither of them heard me.

"Murderess," said Chris. "Shall I spell that, too?" He was standing facing Aunt Maria. She was in her afternoon chair with her hands on both her sticks, staring. She looked hurt and helpless, as anyone would, when Chris went on. "You killed Dad, because he found out about the green box and tried to get it back, didn't you? I don't know what you did to him, except I know he didn't go off the cliff like everyone was supposed to think—"

"How dare you!" said Aunt Maria. "I've never killed anything in all my life, you poor misguided—"

"You did for him somehow. Same difference," Chris interrupted. "I know you did. And you did for Lavinia, because she knew too much. And—"

"Stop," said Aunt Maria, in a feeble, warning way. "Stop there!"

"No, I shan't," said Chris. "You cover it up with deafness and politeness all the time, but it's true. It's the green box, isn't it? Long before Dad and Lavinia, you got rid of Antony Green in order to get hold of that box and the power in—"

Aunt Maria stood up then, with no difficulty at all. "I've heard enough," she said. She pointed the rubber end of one of her sticks at Chris. The other she held ready to thump on the floor. "By the power vested in me," she said, "go on four feet in the shape your nature makes you, young man." Truly she said that, and she thumped the second stick on the carpet.

And Chris—Chris gave a sort of wail and folded up as if the pointing stick had hit him in the middle. I remember the way the palms of his hands hit the floor and then sort of shrank and bent, so that he was holding himself mostly on his eight fingers. His thumbs went traveling up his arms, shrinking and growing a curved pinkish nail each. The rest of him was a quick seething, too quick to watch. He didn't grow much smaller. That surprises me still. He just seethed into a different thing, with pink flesh boiling into gray and brown and yellowish hair, and his own hair getting swallowed under big growing ears. His clothes fell off about then. The thing he was growing into snarled and fought and backed wildly away from the jeans and the sweater, and bent a head with long white teeth in it to tear at the pants clinging to its back legs. There was a thickish gray tail under the pants.

The kitchen door slammed open. Elaine stood there. "You haven't done it again!" she said.

The thing that was Chris backed away from her with the lips of its muzzle up to show its teeth. He looked like a smallish Alsatian dog by then.

I saw Elaine's face as she first saw him, and I swear she was almost crying. "Is it a wolf?" she said, sort of hoarse and loud.

Aunt Maria leaned on her sticks and inspected Chris. "I think so," she said. He was cowering back against the table to keep away from her. "He richly deserved it," she said.

Chris panicked then and raced round the room, long and low, trying to get away. He made one dart at the doorway, saw me, and headed the other way. I dodged back from the door into the hall. Partly it was the sight of his face with its panic-staring, light-colored wolf eyes. He was an animal, but he still looked like Chris. Partly I wanted to get the front door open and let him get away, but my knees were weak, and I had to lean against the wall. There were crashings and rushings from the dining room and I heard Aunt Maria say, "Open the window. Chase it out."

Elaine said, "I'm damned if I want to get bitten, if you do! It's wild!" Then there was a bang and she swore and the kitchen door crashed. I think she'd left the back door open and Chris got out that way. I heard her say, "It's gone. Good riddance. Now what do you tell its mother, for goodness' sake?"

That was when I realized that none of them had seen me, except Chris for that split second. They were too occupied, too violent, somehow. I crept to the stairs and sat there, holding the banister. I was shaking. I couldn't believe what I'd seen. I still can't.

Aunt Maria said, "Dear Betty. So understanding. No trouble at all, dear."

"If you say so," Elaine sort of grunted. "What of little sister? Where's she?"

"Upstairs, dear," said Aunt Maria. "I think she knows about the box, but that's all. No harm done. Do try to stop crying, dear. These things happen. He was getting far too dangerous, you know."

"I'd gathered that," Elaine said. "Do you take me for a fool?" She sniffed and coughed and asked, "Are you going to want me here?"

"Sit with me," said Aunt Maria. "I feel tired. You can help with dear Betty."

I crawled upstairs very softly on hands and knees and sat in Chris's room on the floor, trying to imagine the same low-down view that Chris would get of it now. All Chris's arrangements were there. The fishing line had torn the curtain and the thermometer had fallen on the floor, but they were a person's arrangements, clever things to do. I wondered what it would feel like to be Chris now. Then I thought, No! I must have imagined it. Or maybe she'll turn him back before Mum realizes. And I still found it almost impossible to believe.

The Mrs. Urs made it even harder to believe. I wasn't going to go downstairs at first, when the doorbell rang.

"Naomi, dear!" Aunt Maria shouted. "Answer the door, dear!"

And Elaine yelled, "Don't bother. *I'm* here. I'll do it."

Then I realized I didn't dare stay upstairs or they'd realize I knew about Chris. I didn't want to turn into a wolf, too. So I went down. Elaine, who didn't even look as if she'd been crying, let alone chasing a wolf round someone's dining room, was cheerfully showing in a happy group of Zoe Green, Hester Bailey, and Phyllis Forbes. Every one of them made me want to cringe for a different reason, but I went through into the kitchen and turned out the cake Mum had baked. While I did, I thought carefully about the way I usually behaved. When I brought the cake in, I said, "Where's Chris, Auntie?"

"He went out, dear," said Elaine. The literal truth, after all, but the "dear" was unusual. I thought, I must be very careful!

"Remember the silver teapot," said Aunt Maria. "Will you be little mother this afternoon, Naomi, dear?"

So I did the tea and tried to behave as if nothing had happened. The others behaved as if nothing had happened, too.

It was creepy. All polite jolly chatter and everyone saying Aunt Maria looked so well today. I thought they all knew about Chris. Look at the way Elaine knew the moment it happened. But no one gave a sign, and Aunt Maria was just the same as usual. I felt a real traitor to Chris, pretending, too, but the more I think about it, the more I think the best way I can help Chris is by pretending and staying human.

I thought a lot, though. You do when something awful happens. I thought a lot about Dad when the news came that he'd gone over the cliff. Now I thought about Chris and the things he'd hinted at. I thought: It's between women and men in Cranbury, and the women are winning. The green box does it. I looked at Zoe Green's mad, gushing face. She was talking about ectoplasmic manifestations. And I thought, Aunt Maria did for your son. Why are you such friends with her? I looked at Hester Bailey and wondered if she knew all about our old car and Zenobia Bailey. She looked too sensible to have a relation like Zenobia—all brown tweeds and sensible thick stockings—but Aunt Maria is sort of related to us, after all. Then I looked at Phyllis Forbes. She has a pink, shiny face with a pointing nose and short, fairish hair like an old-fashioned schoolgirl. I wondered if she knew that half her orphans had just been irradiated with stuff from that green box. I don't think so. I think only Mr. Phelps knows that and I hope none of them ever finds out.

Mum came in as they were leaving. She looked all pink and fresh and cheerful. "Where's Chris got to?" she said.

"I think he went out, dear," Aunt Maria said vaguely.

"Saw him going down the street," Elaine backed her up.

"I expect he'll be in when he's hungry," Mum said.

She was a bit surprised when supper was ready and Chris still wasn't in, but I backed Aunt Maria up then and I said Chris must have taken the rest of yesterday's cake with him. "He'll be back for bedtime," I said. It went against the grain to back Aunt Maria up, but I'd thought a lot about it, and I know it's easier to make Mum understand when she's not all worked up first. I'm going to tell her at bedtime.

Mum said, “Bother. I wanted to measure him for this new sweater.” And she began to cast on stitches in the pea green wool. “I daresay I can do the back by guess,” she said.

I wish she wasn’t doing that.

sEveN

Mum doesn't believe me.

Last night I waited until Aunt Maria began snoring, then I said, "Mum, you know Chris still hasn't come in."

Mum was sitting up in bed brushing Lavinia. She had the cat on a sheet of newspaper, and she said, "You have to make sure there are no fleas' eggs left—yes, he has, Mig. Don't be silly."

"When did he come in, then?" I said.

"Just now, while we were putting Auntie to bed," Mum said. "You heard him. He called up to say he was taking his supper up to his room."

I snatched up my candle in a flood of relief and went racing down to Chris's room. For a moment I thought Chris *was* there. His bed was in the tumble he always leaves it in and looked as if there was a person there. But I banged my hand down on the biggest lump, and it went flat. Then I put the candle down and pulled the covers off, and the sheet was cold and wrinkled.

"What are you doing, dear?" Aunt Maria called as usual.

"Looking for C—for a book," I said. Then I went into our room. Mum looked up with a smile and a puff of gray hairs in one hand.

"What did I tell you?" she said.

"No, he *isn't*!" I whispered. Aunt Maria hadn't begun snoring again and I didn't dare say any more.

"He's downstairs feeding his face," Mum said, laughing. "I heard him go down. I hope he'll leave *some* bread for breakfast."

I was getting into bed when Aunt Maria finally began snoring. I said, "*Mum*, Chris *isn't* there. I *know* you're going to find that hard to believe—he isn't there because Aunt Maria turned him into a wolf."

Mum shoved Lavinia aside and turned over to go to sleep. "Miggie, love," she said, in her deepest and drowsiest voice, "I'm a bit tired to join in one of your romances at the moment. Just go to sleep."

"It's *true*!" I said. I shook her to make her stay awake. "Mum, Chris is a *wolf*. And I don't know what to *do*!"

"End the story some other way," Mum said. "And Mig . . . shake me once again, and I'll hit you. I'm tired." And she went to sleep.

Well, I thought, she'll *have* to notice in the morning. I lay down and tried to go to sleep, but I couldn't for ages.

I kept wondering where Chris was and how he was managing. To make things worse, it started to rain. I could hear it hammering on the roof. Lavinia came and curled up by my neck, purring. I suppose she was pleased not to be out, but I thought, You selfish beast! *You're* all right! Which was not fair, because I was as selfish as Lavinia and neither of us could help it. I wondered whether to get up and go to the goblin wood and look for Chris. He'd have had to go to the wood. I thought I ought to go and make sure he could get at the pork pie we left under the tree. But I was too scared to try. I told myself that wild animals had coats to protect them from the weather, but wild animals are used to being out in the rain and Chris wasn't. I wondered whether he thought like a wolf, or knew he was Chris really. And I wondered and wondered how I could make Aunt Maria turn him back. I still can't think how. She never did like Chris, anyway.

Today had been awful.

I had forgotten how much of Mum's time Aunt Maria takes up and how she shouts to know what's going on if you talk privately. All I seemed to be able to do was to say, "Look, Mum. Chris hasn't had breakfast."

"Go and dig the lazy creature out," Mum said, flying past with more marmalade.

When she came back, I said, "Chris isn't in his room, and his bed hasn't been slept in."

"I wish he'd remember to make his bed," Mum said. "He's in the living room." Then Aunt Maria called out, and she jumped up. "Tell him to eat something before he goes out," she said, and ran off upstairs again.

When she came down again, I said, "He's not in the living room, Mum. He's a wolf."

"Yes, he does eat a lot," Mum said. "He went out. I heard the front door. I wish he hadn't gone out in the fog."

The fog was down all day, as thick and bluish as Lavinia's fur. I kept thinking of how damp and cold Chris would be. I could see how Lavinia felt. She crouched in the garden shed all day with little drops of water all over her, looking wretched. I kept trying to tell Mum about Chris, and if she didn't think I was talking about something else or writing a story, she seemed to think Chris was in the other room or that he had just gone out.

When she was getting lunch, I shut the kitchen door so Aunt Maria wouldn't hear and said, "Mum, *listen* to me. *Chris is a wolf*. Understand? That's why he's not here. He hasn't been here since yesterday afternoon."

"Don't be silly, Mig," Mum said. "He took a packed lunch and went out. You know he did."

She hadn't mentioned packed lunch before. I said, "When did he take the packed lunch?"

"It must have been while we were getting Auntie dressed," Mum said. "He used all the white bread up."

"No. *We* finished the white loaf at breakfast," I said.

"Then he must have taken brown bread," Mum said. "Mig, if you're going to hang around in here, peel the potatoes while I do the sprouts."

I think it was then that it dawned on me that Mum wasn't going to notice Chris was missing. She has been made so that she thinks Chris is just round the corner all the time. She doesn't realize that she never sees him. I don't know why I didn't understand earlier. If Aunt Maria can turn Chris into a wolf, she's surely strong enough to do this to Mum—except that it seems a different kind of thing, much more natural and ordinary, and I didn't really think she could do both kinds.

And that made me understand, too, that Aunt Maria was quite capable of turning a person into a cat, as well. I didn't do the potatoes. I went outside into the gray-white garden and walked up to the shed, getting soaked with fog drops from the bushes. Lavinia was crouching in a corner of the shed. She mewed miserably at me.

"*Are* you Lavinia really?" I said. "Mew three times if you are." And I waited. The cat stared at me with flat yellow eyes and went on staring. It was just a cat and a rather stupid one at that. But it *could* be Lavinia. In which case, Chris probably doesn't know he's Chris, either. He'll be a wild wolf even to himself and I'll have to capture him, somehow, to get him turned back. He'll bite. It will be terrible. Oh, heavens, how I wish this really was a story I was writing! I'd write in a happy ending this moment. But it isn't, it's real, and it goes on and on.

Over lunch I realized Aunt Maria was talking as if Mum and I were staying with her for good. She kept saying things like, "Don't leave the spring cleaning any later than May, will you, dear? I usually have all the curtains washed then, but you needn't bother. They can wait till you've some time in summer." Then she said, "I'd like little Naomi to be confirmed this autumn. I'll telephone the vicar."

"Mum!" I whispered when we were washing up. "We aren't going to stay here with Aunt Maria, are we?"

"I'm beginning to think it's the only thing we can do," Mum said. "Lavinia's obviously gone for good, and Auntie is quite helpless on her own."

"But what about your job? And Chris and I have to go to school in two weeks," I said. I keep reminding her about Chris. She takes no notice.

"We can settle schools here," Mum said. "I'll have to give up my job of course." You wouldn't believe how cheerfully she said it.

My back crept—it was like a cold hand on the back of my neck—as I realized how deeply Aunt Maria has been at work on Mum. "Mum," I said. "She's *not* helpless. You said so yourself. Put her in a home."

"Mig! What an unkind thought! She'd be miserable away from the things she's always known," Mum said.

"So am I miserable away from the things *I've* always known!" I said. "Mum, I want to go home."

"You're only a little girl," Mum said, laughing. "You'll adapt."

It's like trying to fight the fog outside. The fog had one blessing, though. No Mrs. Urs turned out in it except Benita Wallins. She sat with her fat bandaged legs stretched out across the carpet and said to me, "I hear you're always writing away. Going to be a journalist, are you, dear?"

"I'm going to write famous books," I said.

B. Wallins laughed. She is the jolliest of all the Mrs. Urs, but when she laughs you feel she has just called you a bad name.

"I learn the art from other famous writers," I said, like replying to an insult. "I know hundreds of poems and things."

"Let's hear one then," said Benita W. unbelievingly.

"In my young days we were all taught to recite," Aunt Maria said. "Stand up properly, dear, and hold your head up as you speak."

I don't think they thought I could. So I stood up and recited my very favorite poem, called "The Battle of Lepanto." It is ever so long. I know it all. It is full of splendid things like "The cold Queen of England is looking in the glass" and "risen from a doubtful seat and half-attained stall/The last knight of Europe takes weapons from the wall." I got quite carried away by that bit, where Don John of Austria goes to war where none of the other kings will. I wish there was a Last Knight of Europe here in Cranbury to come to our aid. But the only one I can think of is Mr. Phelps.

There was a chilly silence when I had finished. Aunt Maria said, "What a clever little memorizer you are, dear. Don't you know anything more suitable?"

I shan't recite another word for her. No, on second thought, I *shall*. "Tam O'Shanter." That is all about witches, but my Scottish accent isn't very good.

In the middle of the night, Chris came and howled in the garden.

I didn't hear him straight away. What woke me up was Lavinia, digging all her claws into me with terror. She had gone like bent steel knitting needles inside a ball of wool, she was so frightened. I rolled over wondering, What's scared her *now*? Then I heard it. It is the most unearthly, eerie noise, a wolf howling. It turned my stomach and stood my hair up in prickles. I thought, *the ghost!* and dived under the covers like Lavinia.

Then I heard the thin yodeling wail again and realized what it was. I think there is something built into the genes of the human race that tells them a wolf is howling, even though the last wolf in Britain was shot two hundred years ago.

I jumped out of bed. Shut up, you fool! I thought. You'll wake Elaine, and she'll make Larry shoot you with his rabbit gun! I was so terrified of Elaine that I forgot to think of ghosts or be scared in the dark. The howl came again as I got to the stairs, and I felt as if I'd taken wings. I pelted into Chris's room in the dark and dodged his table with the lamp on it almost without noticing and got to the window.

Chris's room is over the kitchen, so it sticks out into the garden. The fog had gone, leaving a clear dark blue night and a moon riding furiously through the clouds. I could see Chris quite clearly standing in the middle of the lawn. He was a pale spindly dog shape, higher on the legs than an Alsatian, with a small pointed head. He was raising his head to give another howl. I wrestled frantically to get the window open and stop him.

He heard me. I saw his head tilt as his ears caught the noise. You forget how sharp an animal's ears are. And I think he was waiting, hoping I'd hear. I had no sooner pushed the window up than he started to gallop toward the house, faster and faster. First I was frightened. Then I realized what he meant to do, and I got out of the way of the window just in time. There is a sloping coal bin on the end of the kitchen, to which Chris has staggered back and forth with coal for nearly two weeks now. I heard the strong thump of paws on its wooden lid, then

Chris was half through the window. He nearly missed with his back legs and had to scrabble for a bit, and I was just going to pull him. But he made it and bounded down to the floor, pushing himself against me and making little whining noises.

"Oh, Chris!" I said. "I *am* glad to see you!"

He is miserable. I could tell that at once. His coat was still damp from the rain and the fog, and I know he was freezing for a day and a night. But it is more than that. It is a kind of shame. He knows he is a wolf and he hates it. He hates the strong way he smells when he is wet. I could tell that because he kept breaking off whining all the time I was lighting the lamp, to give himself disgusted little licks. He hates having a tail. He turned round and bit his tail when I'd got the lamp going, to show me.

"I know," I said. "But I can't think of any way to make her turn you back." He knew that. He looked at me as if he'd expected it, resigned to misery. Even though he has gray wolf eyes and a black nose, he still looks like Chris, with Chris's expressions in his face. He is a very young, skinny, forlorn wolf. "Are you hungry?" I said. His ears pricked. He was starving. I'm not sure he could bring himself to kill things and eat them raw.

There were no more cookies in the flower basket, so we had to creep downstairs. I was terrified Aunt Maria would wake up, but she never did. I think she sleeps much more soundly toward the middle of the night. She never woke up the night I ran away from the ghost, either.

In the kitchen, Chris drank a bowl of milk—he did it very noisily and badly; I could see he was not used to lapping yet—while I fetched out all the loose food I could find. He nosed aside the lettuce, but he ate everything else, even a tomato. He ate raw sausages, raw bacon, a frozen hamburger, cold Yorkshire pudding and a lump of cheese.

"Are you sure this won't make you ill?" I whispered.

He shook his head and looked up hopefully. He was still hungry. I tried him with cornflakes then, but he sneezed them all over the floor. Wolves don't seem to get on with cornflakes. So I found the sardines Mum had got for Lavinia and a lot of cake. Chris gobbled it all, while I crawled about sweeping up cornflakes and making sure no paw-prints showed on the linoleum. I'm used to that with Lavinia.

Chris did a wonderful stretch then, rocking back with his forepaws straight out and then standing up slowly, so that the stretch traveled the whole way down his body and out at each back leg in turn. Then he shook, to show me he felt better. His coat fluffed up, quite thick and almost glossy. He is not really gray, more brindled, with darker hair on top and yellower hair underneath, and the colors mostly mixed together on the rest of him. He jerked his head to say, Come with me, and went trotting swift and busy through the dining room. I heard him softly loping upstairs as I switched out the kitchen light and groped after.

It's all right for you, you can see in the dark! I thought. Wait for me.

I was sure he was going to jump through the window of his room again. But when I got to the room he was on the bed, lying on his side with all four long thin legs sticking over the edge, looking at me pleadingly. He was terribly tired and sick of being alone.

"All right," I said. "I'll stay with you." Actually, I hadn't realized how much I'd missed Chris until I thought he was leaving again. I was going to ask him to stay. So I left the window open so that he could get away when he wanted and hauled the covers off the floor and wrapped them round both of us. Chris put his narrow muzzle on my knee, heaved a great sigh, and went to sleep. Animals are good at doing that. And Chris has always been good at sleeping.

I stayed awake for a long time, guarding him. If you look at wolves in a zoo, you will see that they always leave one of the pack awake on guard. That made it a bit like when we were small, and I was afraid of the dark. Chris used to guard me. I stroked him sometimes, as if he was a dog. He is awfully thin. I could feel all his ribs through his coat, and his hipbones were like knives. Perhaps wolves are always that thin. His fur is soft inside by the skin but much harsher on the outside. Anyway, he didn't like me poking at him and shrugged crossly till I stopped. He got beautifully warm and I suppose that made me go to sleep. I don't remember turning the lamp out, but I must have done. It was out when I woke up.

All this time I had clean forgotten the ghost. I sort of remembered in the middle of a dream I had, but then the dream became too horrible to remember anything else. It started with a smell of earth and growing things. I could hear grass and leaves rustling, and I thought, I'm somewhere out-of-doors! But that wasn't quite right, because the rustling was overhead somewhere, as if there was a tree growing on the roof. I was terribly cold, so I thought, I must be outside. Then somebody's feet ran over the top, where the tree was growing, with a kind of solid booming. And I realized I was buried in the earth.

It went on for years, too. Sometimes I struggled and shouted. Nobody heard me, and I could hardly move. Sometimes I lay with chill cloggy earth all round me and despaired. This went on so long that I panicked. I shouted and raged and struggled and cried. When that happened, I could tell that great storms came in from the sea. I could hear the wind shouting and hail threshing the trees overhead, and sometimes one cracked and broke. I could tell that long lines of storm clouds went out from me, far inland, and made havoc in places I had never seen. And after years and years, I thought, If I know this and can do all that, then I ought to have strength to get out of here. So I began working, working, slowly and patiently, to get free. I had almost found out how, when I woke up and found a dim streetlight sort of light in the room.

I was so glad to be out of the earth that it didn't strike me as at all frightening when I saw a man in the room beside the open window. He didn't seem a frightening sort of man, anyway. I had fallen asleep leaning one shoulder against the wall, so I was sitting up, with a good view of him. He was odd-looking. He had a small, pointed face with a lot of swept-back hair and very thick dark eyebrows that bent in two upside-down Vs like a clown's eyebrows. His whole face was kind of quirked and crooked and surprised-looking. When I first saw him, he was drumming all his fingers on the edge of a bookshelf and rubbing his pointed chin, puzzled, as if he'd forgotten what he'd come for. Then he nodded. He'd remembered. He turned and came toward the bed. He leaned down, quite near me, and I saw he wanted to speak to Chris.

Oh, it's the ghost! I thought. From the side he had a little hooked nose, like an owl's beak. Or a parrot's. A cross between a court jester and a parrot, I thought. It was a good description, but he was nicer than that.

Chris was curled up in a skinny doughnut shape

against my knees. But he came awake the instant the man bent over him. He raised his head, with the pointed ears pricked, and gave a miserable little whine.

The man stopped with one hand stretched out that had been going to shake Chris. He hadn't realized until that minute that Chris was a wolf. He stood like that, staring at Chris, and his face twisted even more with a sort of horrified sympathy. Then his hand flopped in a helpless way, and he started to turn away.

"No, wait!" I said. "You can say it to me. And Chris understands."

The man whirled round and stared at me. He seemed not to have known I was there till then. One of his clown eyebrows went up and he put his hand up again in a sort of fending-off way.

"It's all right," I said. "I know I'm a girl, but I'm not on their side. I'm not even neutral now she did this to Chris. Who are you? Do you know what we can do?"

For a moment I thought he was going to speak. His face sort of gathered to make a word. Then he shook his peculiar maned head and smiled. He meant, Sorry, not to you. It was a huge, wide smile, as odd as the rest of him, one long line of smile wrapped most of the way round his face. I know that kind of smile from Chris. Chris uses it to get out of trouble with.

"I'm not trouble, honestly," I said.

But he was fading by then. I could see books through

him, all except his smiling face. That sort of winked out and the light went with it. All I could see was the outline of Chris standing up on all four legs, whining a little, against the window.

"Chris," I said, "would he know how to get you changed back?" Chris turned and pushed his nose at me and pushed again. "All right," I said. "I'll come here tomorrow night and try to make him speak. Hadn't you better go now?"

Chris pushed his nose at me and bounded to the window. For a moment he teetered in the opening. I think his wolf's muscles knew they could jump to the coal shed easily, but Chris's mind didn't. Then he jumped, *scrape, thump,* and he was gone, too. I went drearily back to my own cold side of Mum's bed, sniffing a little. I feel quite helpless. I suppose that's what the dream was about.

Eight

This morning I made Chris's bed, so that I could show Mum it hadn't been slept in. The room smelled of wolf slightly, which is a bit like dog but not quite.

When I showed her, Mum smiled her fond smile. "So he made his bed for once, did he? Or did someone else I know make it for him? You shouldn't spoil him, Mig." Then she sent me out shopping. "Chris has eaten all the food again," she said. She didn't seem to realize he must have eaten it raw.

I walked down the neat empty windswept seafront. There was Mr. Phelps, striding back from his swimming in all weathers. I tried to stop him. "Please, Mr. Phelps—" He just walked straight past, staring into the distance with his fanatical eyes.

I went sadly down onto the sand and walked along watching the waves crashing. The sea looked thick, bare, strong, and real. It seemed far more reasonable than anything else in Cranbury. But it isn't really reasonable, I suppose, if you think of the moon pulling all that water up and down like a yo-yo every tide. Perhaps life is all like that, full of terrible hidden unreasonableness.

It was good to have peace to think. Aunt Maria talks and shouts so in the house that my mind is never quiet. I thought of everything that had happened, and it seemed to me that I might be beginning to see a way of doing something. But not quite. A wave bashed down across my shoes. The tide was coming in, and I felt helpless again and went shopping.

Chris must have felt even more helpless and frustrated that day. I suppose he thought he had nothing to lose.

Anyway, Mum had spent the morning washing. She washed Chris's things, including the clothes that dropped off him when he became a wolf, and didn't notice that left him with nothing he could have been wearing. She also washed a row of Aunt Maria's petticoats and mighty blue Baghdads. She pinned the lot out on the line and left them merrily flapping in the wind.

"But, dear, you can see them from the dining-room window," said Aunt Maria. "I can't have my friends sitting and watching such things."

Mum protested it was a lovely drying day. In vain. As soon as the doorbell rang for the first Mrs. Urs I was sent out into the garden to take all the washing in. I did it very slowly. It was such a silly thing to worry about.

But then if I wore blue Baghdads I wouldn't want my friends to know, either. I said so to Lavinia. She was sitting in the ornamental ferns, watching. I got about half the clothes down and folded them in a basket.

I said to Lavinia, "I suppose I'm not doing this the way you used to, am I?"

But she stared past me and bolted, a long low streak of gray. I looked round, expecting to see Elaine looming over her wall, telling me to get those Baghdads down at once. And it was Chris. He was standing on the back wall, the way he must have come in the night, sort of laughing down at me with his tongue flopping.

"Oh, no, go away," I said. "Don't be a fool. All the Mrs. Urs are here."

I suppose that was what he wanted to know. He jumped down into the garden at once, in a lovely limber flowing leap. He's getting better at being a wolf. He can move like lightning. Before I could move at all, he had jumped past me up at the clothesline and landed with a pair of blue Baghdads between his teeth. Then he made for the back door. I had left it open, of course. And the kitchen door opens into the dining room if you shove it. Chris knew that. So I didn't follow him. I went to the dining-room window and looked in.

It was wonderful. Chris was galloping round and round the crowded room trailing the blue Baghdads. The silver teapot had fallen over on its side and was raining hot tea on the carpet. At least one cup was smashed. Everyone was yelling and screaming, and Aunt Maria was waving both sticks in the air. Zoe Green was standing on a chair with her hands together and her eyes shut. I think she was praying. The rest of them were making feeble efforts to stop Chris by grabbing the Baghdads. Just as I looked, Benita Wallins did grab them. Chris simply jerked his head contemptuously sideways and tore them out of her hands. Benita Wallins tipped over backward, with her fat legs in the air. She wears Baghdads, too, pink ones.

Chris galloped over to the table then. He put out a paw and swept the cake off onto the floor. Then he stood with one forefoot on the cake and the Baghdads trailing from his mouth, daring them all to get it. Only Mum was brave enough to try. She edged forward, both hands out, and I could see her mouth saying, "Nice doggie. Good dog then." Chris stared at her intently. I could see he was hoping she would recognize him, but she didn't.

All the while, Aunt Maria was screaming, "Get it out of here! Get it out of sight! Oh—*Oh*—OH!"

This seemed to brace the younger Mrs. Urs. They really do defend Aunt Maria. Corinne West and Phyllis West and Adele Taylor between them pulled the tea-soaked tablecloth off the table from under the teacups. They held it by a corner each and came tiptoeing toward Chris, like bullfighters, all in their neat pleated skirts and shiny shoes. They tried to drop it over Chris.

There was absolute chaos for a moment. The tablecloth surged, and neatly dressed ladies plunged in all directions. I saw Adele Taylor step on the cake and go skating into Zoe Green's chair. The two of them ended up madly clinging to each other. In the midst of it, Chris must have trodden in the pool of hot tea. I heard an agonized howl, even above Aunt Maria's screaming. But Mum's instincts are all right underneath. She went sideways, sliding her back round the wall, and opened the door to the hall so that Chris could get away.

The side door into the garden crashed. I whizzed away from the window and looked round the corner of the kitchen by the coal shed. Elaine came marching up the side passage and stormed in through the back door. Whoops! I thought. As soon as she was inside, I raced out through the garden door into the street. I had to get the front door open, somehow, and let Chris get out. I thought if I rang the bell, someone would have to come to see who I was.

But Mum got the front door open as I got there. Chris shot out past her into the street. Somehow, in the middle of the bullfight, his head had gone into one of the great baggy legs of the blue Baghdads. There were holes torn in it, but he was almost completely blinded. I saw one wild staring wolf eye as he dashed past. Mum leaned round the door and saw me.

"Help it, Mig!" she shrieked above the screams coming from the house. "Take those off it!"

Mrs. Urs came running out past her into the street. Adele Taylor was waving an umbrella, Corinne West had a golf club, and Benita Wallins came puffing after, flapping an empty plastic bag. I saw Miss Phelps's lace curtain fluttering as I pelted down the street after Chris.

He was running on three legs, pawing at the Baghdads with one front foot. His other three legs kept treading on the rest of the Baghdads. Every so often, he stopped and backed round in an angry circle, trying to back out of it all. His tail and back were all bushed out with fury. Even so, he ran twice as fast as I could.

"Stop! Wait! I'll get it off you!" I yelled.

Maybe he was too upset to hear. Near the end of the street, his other front leg trod hard on the trailing blue cloth and he nearly pitched on his nose. But that tugged the elastic back across his head. I saw his ears come popping out. He went galloping down the seafront with the Baghdads flapping round his neck like a mad blue collar.

I ran along the front after him. People kept coming out of the houses to shout and wave and look. I saw more people in Cranbury in that half hour than I have seen all the rest of the time we've been here. Most of them were women, but there were quite a few old men and one or two men in seaboots who were not so old.

Chris veered away from them and leaped down on the sand, where the tide was going out again. I saw him, more and more distant, in a crazy outline against the breakers, galloping, stumbling, turning in circles, and stopping to rub himself against rocks. Halfway along the bay, he managed to tear the Baghdads off. They fell into the sea and surged back and forth there. After that Chris sprinted for his life, running like greyhounds do — doubled up, then spread, then doubled up again. He vanished up the sand long before I got to the Baghdads, and the few people who were running after him in front of me gave up and went back to their houses.

I looked at the torn blue bloomers washing to and fro and decided to take them home as a trophy of Chris's protest. I suppose he did it because he had nothing to lose. And he must have hoped Mum would know him. I don't like to think how he feels now he knows she didn't. He'd have had to cross the road and the railway, too, to get back to the woods. I hope he went carefully.

But if he knew the trouble he'd caused! Aunt Maria has had some kind of seizure and been put lovingly to bed by a crowd of Mrs. Urs. All the other ones have come here to make sure she is all right, and Hester Bailey has taken Zoe Green home. Zoe Green has been sitting staring at the wall saying, "A jahudgement, thad's whad it is!" over and over. The other Mrs. Urs keep going on about "The terrible great dog. What a shock to your auntie!" I wanted to say, "Aunt Maria got what she deserved," but I didn't dare.

Elaine is marching up and down through the house, booming orders. We have had the doctor. He is a zombie like the men on the train, a soft gray one in a striped suit. The vicar has just arrived. He is Phyllis West's bachelor brother. I don't think he is a zombie, but I think he doesn't understand.

Mum and I have been flying about looking after Aunt Maria, obeying Elaine's orders, clearing up, and making half a hundred more cups of tea for everyone. While I was kneeling in the dining room with a bucket and cloth, washing the tea Chris spilled out of the carpet, the zombie doctor came and spoke to me. He crouched down beside me. He is a soft and considerate zombie. "Tell me," he said. "You were here. Was there really a dog?"

I looked at my hands all brown and shiny with tea. "She didn't just imagine it, if that's what you think," I said. "It was . . . a sort of Alsatian."

"Thank you," he said. "I know you're very busy, but would you mind going to the drugstore with this prescription? Now, before he shuts."

So I wiped off the tea and took the prescription. I looked at it first. He is Dr. Bailey. That part was printed but the rest of it was in doctor writing and I couldn't read a word. The druggist is A. C. Taylor. It said on the bottle. I think he is Adele Taylor's zombie. He is skin and bone with three streaks of hair. He knew all about it. "Terrible business," he said. "Needs a sedative, does she? I won't keep you two minutes." He went off into his cubbyhole that says prescriptions, smiling and humming a dull little tune. I wondered if he knew his wife had stepped on a cake. But I got bored waiting. Mr. zombie Taylor seemed to be telephoning while he counted pills. So I went to the door and tried to think.

It was dark outside by then, but I saw our old car as it shot past. It was just a glimpse, but I know now I'd know it anywhere. I stared after it and thought, What a fool I am! There *is* something I can do! Then Mr. Taylor called out that the pills were ready. I walked home feeling cross with myself. I pride myself on having ideas, but all the time we've been in Cranbury, I've been letting Chris do all the real active thinking. Perhaps it's because Chris is a year older than me. But I am not usually like this. I think it is the way everyone here takes for granted that having ideas is not women's work and not nice, somehow. In future, I swear to do better.

Chris didn't come back last night. He must have had enough in the afternoon. He'll be very hungry when he does come.

I left the window of his room open when I went to bed. Mum went to sleep quickly, with Lavinia round her neck the way Aunt Maria wears her dead fox. I got up stealthily and went to Chris's room. I am not afraid of ghosts anymore. I got into Chris's bed and went to sleep there. If Mum asked, I was going to say that Chris's bed was empty, so why should I share? But she didn't even ask in the morning. She seems to be slowly forgetting Chris exists.

I had the dream again. I remember now that Chris said the ghost brought dreams. I looked up where I wrote it down. It was as bad as last time, only realler somehow. I could feel the clammy clods of earth round me when I tried to move. This time I tried to believe I was Chris sleeping in the cold woods among the goblin trees. But I could tell, somehow, that they were a different kind of trees growing on top of me, lighter and bushier. And I fought to get out harder than ever.

Then I sort of burst through and sat up to find the room full of pale light. Sweat was pouring down me. The ghost was standing looking at me, thoughtfully, with a hand holding his chin. He looked like a scarecrow. He was wearing a long green coat that looked as if it had been left out in a field for a year. I could see grass and mud and cowpats sticking to it. His face is a bit like a carved turnip, anyway. When he saw I was awake, one of the V-shaped eyebrows slid up. He doesn't take me seriously the way he does Chris.

"That's not fair!" I said. "I need your help. Please! You know what's happened to Chris—"

He smiled his long, long grin and just faded away.

I was so angry I threw Chris's pillow at where he had been. It nearly went out of the window—luckily it didn't. It was raining again. Poor Chris.

It is raining this morning, too, and Lavinia is crouched in the shed. I don't blame Mum for not being able to think of Chris. The telephone never stops ringing. The whole of Cranbury is asking after Aunt Maria. And Aunt Maria is not dead. I rather hoped she would be and Chris would turn back into Chris the moment the last breath left her body. No way. Aunt Maria is sitting on her roped morning sofa, shouting, "Betty! Telephone, dear!" every time the phone rings, just as if Mum couldn't hear it, too. I hate her. I really do.

And it is rather frightening. Everyone talked about Chris as if he was a dog yesterday. Today they are talking about "the wolf."

"Tell them it must have escaped from a zoo somewhere, dear!" Aunt Maria calls to Mum. And she knows where the wolf came from even better than I do. I *must* warn Chris not to do anything in daytime again. I hope he comes tonight.

Nine

The Mrs. Urs made me sick this afternoon. They sat in an anxious circle round Aunt Maria asking how she was after her terrible experience. They were all there, even Elaine. They all must know about Chris—I'm *sure* they do—but none of them seemed to care at all about *his* terrible experience. It was all Aunt Maria and had their dear queen bee been harmed. Mum is right about her being queen bee. The zombies are her drones. I suppose that makes the clones into bee grubs waiting to hatch. I wonder if they are.

I sat thinking this with my chin on my chest, looking at all their pairs of legs as they sat—fat legs, skinny legs, legs with purple scaly patches, smart legs in nice tights, and Mum's legs in jeans. And mine in blue tights with wrinkles at the knees. Twenty-six legs, making thirteen of us, all female. As soon as I realized that, I wanted to go away.

"You loog dired, dear!" Zoe Green said to me. "You

shouldn't. Your ztar is in the azzendand juzt dnow."

"I'm very well, thank you," I said. She looked at me in a puzzled way, wondering why I was being so icy polite. I don't think she realizes.

Then Corinne West said, "Poor Phyllis Forbes sends her apologies. Something terrible seems to have happened at the orphanage. That wolf came out of the woods and savaged one of those poor little children."

I thought, Oh, *no*! Everyone else exclaimed a bit, then Aunt Maria said, "It was bound to happen, with a savage beast like that on the loose. Isn't anybody doing anything about it?"

One of them said, "We should hold a meeting about it."

"Yes," said Aunt Maria. "We should, dear. Elaine, see about it, dear. Get Larry to organize the men."

"Will do," Elaine said cheerily.

By that time I had had enough. I stood up and said, "I'm suffocating in here, Mum. Is it all right if I go out for a bit?"

Elaine looked at me suspiciously, but Aunt Maria said, "That's right, dear. You look pale. Go out and get some fresh air."

The fresh air was full of little drops of rain, but I didn't care. It was one of those times when it seems suddenly warmer outside than indoors. The rain gave the sea a gentler smell than usual. There was the gluey bud smell in the air and even a smell of flowers. You couldn't see the sea for the white mist of rain over it. I wandered about sniffing, thinking maybe Chris hadn't had such a bad time in the woods if it was like this.

They arranged the meeting about him while I was out. The reason I'm writing this now is that Aunt Maria has gone in her dead fox and wheelchair procession to the town hall. I keep hoping Chris will have the sense to come here while they're all discussing him. I don't know what they'll decide, but I know I must warn him. So I keep turning to the window in case he's in the garden. Lavinia digs her claws in every time I do, because I slope her then, and she starts to slide down my skirt. I'll put her out the window when I hear them coming back.

But I wasn't just walking round Cranbury for my health all afternoon. I walked, the way Chris did, so that people would see me going in all directions. The Mrs. Urs were all with Aunt Maria, but I am sure they are just her main women. The way the lace curtains quiver as you pass, she must have the whole town watching for her. I walked past every house in the place before I pretended to go back. Instead, I dodged into the vegetable plots, the way we had done before, and got very wet and prickled walking up beside the hedge to the station car park.

It was worth it. The old blue car that used to be ours was waiting there again. It was in a much more convenient position, too, backed right against the iron railing. I didn't even need to climb over before I took out the kitchen knife I'd picked up on my way out and dug it under the back lock.

It wasn't locked. Either Chris had broken it last time or someone hadn't locked it. The hatch went up so quickly that I nearly didn't catch it before it reared up over the roof and showed the booted porter someone was opening a car. The difficult bit was climbing in while holding the door and then shutting it from inside. I ought to have been good at it. Dad was always going off with both sets of keys. But I'd lost the knack and the door soared away twice before I remembered how to hold it.

I sat in the back beside the toffee for a bit. Then I changed my plan and crawled forward over the back-seat and sat in the front passenger seat. Whoever got into the car might as well know at once that I was there. I felt in the hiding place in case anything was there, but there was nothing. Zenobia Bailey's perfume was still in the air, but not as strong as last time. I sat waiting and planned what I would say to Zenobia if she unlocked the door and climbed in. Then I planned what I'd say if it wasn't Zenobia who got in.

It was not quite dark when the train came. When I heard it clattering and squealing I deliberately lay back and slid down a bit to stop myself going all strung-up and frightened. But it was hard not to be frightened when the footsteps began to crunch on the gravel and car doors banged all round as the zombies got in their cars and drove away. I concentrated on counting how many cars put headlights on and how many didn't, and I got so taken up with that that I almost didn't notice a man was unlocking the car door until he opened it and got in.

He was so much a zombie that he didn't notice me at all. He just sat down and began clattering away at the starter. When I said, "Hello, Dad," his head almost hit the roof.

He turned round. He stared. He looked quite bewildered. He said, "Who . . . what?" Then, in his usual way, he got angry. "What the *hell* do you think *you're* doing here?" he said.

Dad uses anger to cover up all his other feelings. I took no notice and grinned. "Waiting for you," I said. "I got in through the back as usual. Why are you here when you're supposed to be dead?"

"Dead?" he said angrily. "Dead?"

He always pretends not to understand, but I think he really didn't when I explained, "The car was found at the bottom of Cranbury Head, but you weren't in it. Mum thinks you were killed."

"This car?" he said in the same angry way. "*This* car? But I've had it all along!"

"I know," I said. "I think the car crash was some kind of illusion. You really ought to tell Mum you're still alive. It's awfully awkward for her."

"Yes," he said. "I suppose it would be." That sounds reasonable, but it wasn't quite. He always talks about Mum in a half-laughing, sarcastic way. I was watching him carefully. He hadn't changed much. There was the zombie look, but he still looked rather like me if I were three sizes bigger. "And is that why you're here?" he said in the same sarcastic way. "Soul-searching, happy-ending-seeking Mig."

"No," I said. "I've had enough of people pretending and managing one another and being dishonest. I might have used that as an excuse if I wanted to manage you, but I don't. I've come about the green box."

"Green box!" he said. He ran his hands through his hair and looked at the car roof. "Is this another of your stories or something?"

I gave him time to notice that I did know about this green box. I said, "Do you live with Zenobia Bailey these days?"

Dad stopped with both hands in his hair and looked at me. "That's enough, Mig. One way of managing people is to tell them you're being quite honest."

"I *know*!" I said. "Why do people always have to manage one another? Can't they just be people?"

"It doesn't seem to be possible where men and women

are concerned," Dad said, more sarcastic than ever. "You'll learn that, Mig."

"No, I won't," I said. "Tell me about the green box."

Dad just went on as if he hadn't heard me. "That's the real trouble with your mother, Mig. She seemed to think it was possible, too. She was always assuming we thought the same way, and we didn't. You never knew what to expect from her, she was so reasonable! None of the traditional facts seemed to mean anything to her—and she went and taught the same outlook to you and Chris. I tell you, Mig—!"

"You're just working yourself up," I said. "It's all supposed to be over now. Dad, are you under some sort of spell not to tell about the green box?"

I think he may have been. He gave a sort of jump and said, "What the—! What do you mean, green box?"

"Covered all over with peculiar green patterns and full of something strong," I said. "It used to belong to Antony Green. He's dead, isn't he?"

"Poor old Tony," Dad said. "Poor old Tony Green." He sat with his chin down, rather the way I was, staring out at the empty car park. "He and I were at school together," he said. "We used to go off on this same train to school in Minehurst every day, did you know that? He was always the promising one, they all said. I did as well at lessons, but Antony was supposed to be the good-all-round one. Never could make up his mind between science and philosophy and so on. I think he took up archeology when they gave him the green box and told him he was the one who had to stay in Cranbury. I was the one who had to leave. I didn't see the justice of that. I always assumed I would be the one who got the box. Tony didn't value it the way I did."

"How did he die?" I said.

"No idea," Dad said, to my great disappointment. "In fact, I'd always been led to believe he *wasn't* dead—though you'd think he was the way his mother—Zoe Green—took on. It was quite a shock to me when I saw his ghost that night in Aunt Maria's spare room. The ghost spoke to me, said it was looking for the box. Poor old Tony. The box was never there."

"Yes, it was," I said. "You took it."

"Mig, I swear to you I did not," he said. He wasn't angry, so I think he thought he was telling the truth.

"You did," I said, "but it doesn't matter now. What does the box do? What made you decide to stay here and not tell anyone?"

I wish I hadn't asked both those things together. Dad didn't quite answer either, just the way Chris didn't when I asked him about the ghost. He said, "When you meet an old friend you last saw as a skinny teenager, Mig . . . What does it *do*? Well, you'd have one answer and no doubt old Nat Phelps would have another. As I said—"

A Land Rover came hurtling into the car park while he was speaking, so fast that it sprayed mud and pebbles all over the windshield of Dad's car. It skidded to a stop some yards away to the right. Its headlights suddenly made everywhere go dark, and mud ran down the window, but I could see through it enough to see Hester Bailey and Zenobia Bailey jump down from it. They came marching toward Dad's car in an Elaine sort of way.

I got the door open on my side. "I think I'd better be off," I said.

"Yes, you'd better," Dad said. He sounded so nervous I was sorry for him. "Tell Betty I'm still in the land of the living," he said, almost whispering.

"Yes, and you tell them your stomach played up again," I whispered back. "*Don't* say I was here. *Please.*"

"Okay," he said. I think it was a real promise. I hope. He certainly didn't say anything while I was crawling on hands and knees through the muddy gravel and hitching myself through the fence. But then—it's a strange thought—now Dad's been zombied, I think he's as scared of me as he is of Zenobia Bailey.

I heard her open the driver's door and say, "Greg! Whatever is the matter? Mother and I got really worried when you didn't come in."

Dad mumbled something with "stomach" in it.

Hester Bailey said, "If that's all it is, your father can

easily give him something for it." She sounded very relieved.

Zenobia said, "You poor old boy then! Move over and I'll drive."

I crawled and crawled away along the hedge, until my tights and skirt were sopping. I was glad they'd believed Dad. I hadn't meant to get him in trouble, and I didn't want to spoil it by letting them see me. I didn't dare stand up until both cars had driven away. Then I ran back to Aunt Maria's with my teeth chattering and went in through the back door. She always moves back to the dark living room after the Mrs. Urs have gone, so she didn't see me. I had to change all my clothes. Even my sweater was sopping.

"How *did* you get so wet?" said Mum.

"Looking for a way to help Chris," I said. I haven't stopped reminding her. "And by the way, Dad's alive. I just met him."

"You and your happy endings, Mig!" she said, laughing. "You do know that even if he walked in here this moment, nothing would come of it, don't you?"

I thought about it. "Yes," I said. "I do know." When I was little I thought of Mum and Dad as really one person—joined together as Mum-and-Dad—or like the earth and the sky, part of the same view. Now I know they are two separate people who don't get on. The difference between them is that I keep reminding Mum of

Chris, because I know it might do some good. But I didn't even mention Chris to Dad. I knew he'd just cut me off, then get angry and throw me out of the car.

Mum was thinking of Dad, too. She was peeling potatoes on the drain board to let me rinse my muddy tights in the sink. She put her head up with her cheerful, brave look and said, "Just before you were born, Mig, I fell downstairs. *All* the way down. I was terrified in case you'd been harmed. I screamed for Greg. He came, and he looked, and he said, 'That was a stupid thing to do,' and he went away again. I couldn't believe it. But that's what he's like, Mig. It's all right if things are going the way he expects, but if they don't he doesn't want to know."

"I *know*!" I said. I didn't want her to say any more.

She did, though. I suppose she wanted to get him off her chest, too. She said, musingly, "I should have left him then, really. But you were going to be born, and I did hope he'd learn—learn that people aren't just a set of rules, or at least learn that he *could* learn. But he never did, Mig."

Now I'm grateful that Mum said that. It explains the sort of hold Zenobia Bailey must have on Dad. You can see, with every word she says, that Zenobia is the sort of girl who plays by the rules. Dad likes that. I bet she uses the rules just the way Aunt Maria does, to make him feel guilty and do things for her. But he probably expects that. I feel like saying, "Poor old Greg!" the way Dad himself said "Poor old Tony." But I'm very grateful to Dad, too. Now I know who the ghost is. I think that's important.

I can hear them bringing Aunt Maria back. Out, Lavinia. And I *must* warn Chris.

They didn't say what they'd decided, but it sounds as if everyone in Cranbury is going to join in. I did warn Chris, thank goodness.

I slithered down to Chris's room again as soon as Mum was asleep. "Is that you, Naomi?" called Aunt Maria.

"I'm getting a drink of milk, Auntie," I called. "I'm thirsty."

"Is the rug rolled up? Mind you don't slip, dear."

"It *is* rolled up and I'm not ninety!" I shouted. I was cross, because that meant I really did have to go downstairs to the kitchen in the dark, or she would know. So I went down and groped about and fell into things until I found a spare candle. Then I hopefully got out all the loose food to save time later. And off I trudged upstairs.

"Good night, dear!" called Aunt Maria.

That meant I had to go back to the right bed again and climb in with Mum. I went fast asleep, like a log, and I know I would have slept until morning if it hadn't been for Lavinia. She knew Chris was there and tried to get down inside the covers with me in such a clawing hurry that she scratched my arm. I didn't notice the scratch till morning. I just jumped up, half asleep, and went down to Chris's room.

He was standing in the middle of it, ears pricked, waiting for me. I knelt down and hugged him. He wasn't as wet as I expected. He must have found a place to shelter. He put one paw awkwardly across my shoulder to show he was glad to see me, too.

"Oh, Chris!" I said. "That was so stupid with the Baghdads! But it was wonderfully funny, too. Did you see Adele Taylor tread in the cake?"

Chris sort of panted with his tongue lolling. He was laughing.

"But I have to warn you," I said. "They're saying there's a wild wolf escaped from a zoo and it savaged one of the clones. Did you bite a clone?" I put both hands on his furry shoulder blades and looked him in the eyes. "Did you?"

Chris shook his face and stared at me. He meant no, and I knew it was the truth.

"Yes. But they think you're dangerous," I said. "They're going to look for you—try and trap you—tomorrow, I think, maybe both days of the weekend. Promise me you won't do anything like the Baghdads then. Promise me you'll hide. I can't do anything to turn you back if they put you in a zoo."

Chris's ears pricked up at that.

"I'm trying to find out how," I said. "I've been stupid

and only just started to try, but I *promise* I'll get you turned back. But you have to be sensible."

Chris nodded. He put his nose near mine with a rather sad snuffle.

"I know you hate it," I said. "I hate her for doing it. Come downstairs and get some food now."

We went to the kitchen, and Chris ate everything I'd put out. He was starving again. I'm not sure that things like bread and mushroom paté and jam are good for a wolf's digestion, but he ate them. And even though he was starving, he ate neatly and sort of politely. That wasn't Chris. It was wolf. Wolves are very clean, precise creatures, in spite of all the stories. I watched him as he ate, and I thought of all the books that say a person takes on the nature of beast if he's turned into one for too long, and that worried me. I must get him turned back *soon*.

Then we went upstairs again and sat by candlelight on Chris's bed, talking. I mean, I talked. Chris looked and moved his ears and his jaw to show he understood. It was almost just like talking usually—except it wasn't, and I knew Chris was truly miserable.

Next thing I knew, the candle was out, and I was waking out of the dream again, after years of horrible struggling underground. I remember I thought as I woke, I wouldn't like to be that ghost! I didn't know being dead was so awful! And there he was, standing in the middle of the room, faintly lit up. I was sorry for him. The odd thing was, he was looking at us as if he was sorry for *us*. We were in a sort of heap, because we'd both been needing comforting.

I looked up at the funny quirked face of the ghost. Chris looked up with his ears up. Funny! I thought. He looks more old-fashioned than twenty years ago. And he did. The pushed-back mane of hair was like something hundreds of years ago, and the tattered green robe was a bit like a highwayman's coat or something. It was a feeling of king as well as scarecrow and jester he gave you—of someone important dead hundreds of years and half crumbled away. I really did wonder if Dad had told me right.

I said, in rather a wavering voice, "You—you're Antony Green, aren't you? Won't you please speak to us, and tell us how to turn Chris back?"

His face turned to me quite seriously. I got the feeling that he was wondering what he *could* say. But he didn't speak.

"You spoke to Chris and to Dad," I said. "Do you only speak to men? No . . . ," I said, because a sudden idea came to me. "I think you spoke to Lavinia, too. Didn't you? She was downstairs here. She left her nightdress."

He nodded, just a bit humorously, with a sort of comic sadness.

"You mean, everyone you speak to gets done for,

don't they?" I said. "Even after Chris rescued your green box, he got done for. Do you know Mr. Phelps has the green box now? He won't speak to me, either."

He started to smile his wide smile at that. I think the idea of Mr. Phelps with the green box amused him, but I thought it meant he was going away, and I hurried on.

"Oh, *please*!" I said. "I—I think you're in trouble, too. I know you feel awful being dead and buried. If you want your spirit laid to rest or something, I'll do that if you like, in exchange for getting Chris back."

His smile became widely sad at that. He shook his head slightly and seemed to shrug his shoulders, as if he meant, "I give up!" But the smile went quite kind as he faded out.

"Oh, Chris!" I said. "I got it wrong again! I wish you could tell me what he really wants when he comes here. Do you think he'll go and haunt Mr. Phelps now?"

Poor Chris. He can only make gestures just like the ghost. He flapped his tongue against my cheek and went down off the bed, draggingly, ready to jump out the window.

"Remember!" I cried. "You promised. Be careful when they all start looking for you."

I saw his narrow dog-shaped head turn in a sort of nod to me as he jumped. *Thump* went the coal bin. It was a much better jump than last time. He's getting too good at being a wolf.

tEn

Saturday. It seems centuries since I wrote the last bit. It is only three days. It's going to take ages to write down.

Saturday was the day of the hunt.

All the time we were getting Aunt Maria dressed she was saying, over and over, "Now, Betty, you're to stay here with me, dear."

"I always do, don't I?" Mum said, a bit sourly. "What about the kids?"

"I'll let little Naomi go with Elaine and Larry, if she promises to be very good and careful," Aunt Maria said.

Nobody mentioned Chris, I noticed.

Shortly after that, Elaine came tramping in, wearing great green boots below her black mac and a black scarf tied over her head. "We're ready to go," she said. She gave me her two-line smile. "I gather you're coming, too," she said. "You'll need Wellingtons."

How's that for a welcoming invitation?, I thought as

I ran and got my things.

Larry was waiting at the wheel of his car out in the street. It is one of the glossy expensive cars I remember seeing at the station. He didn't say anything of course. And the only thing Elaine said, all the way, was, "I've got a bag of food for you with ours in the back. This may take all day."

Mind you, it wasn't a long way, only to the station car park. I could have walked it. The car park was full when we got there. Someone had opened the gate into the field on the other side of the road, and Larry drove gently, squelchily through it and stopped in a row of cars at the end. There were cars of all shapes and colors, vans, Land Rovers, motorbikes, bicycles. All the cars had their backs open and men were deedily bending over them. I've never seen so many green Wellingtons together in my life. Larry had green Wellingtons, too, and a little tweed hat on. He went and opened the back of his glossy car. When he turned round from it, he was carefully carrying two long guns.

Gray and pink Dr. Bailey came hurrying up to him, also carrying a gun. "We've got a man every fifty feet, all along the fields beyond the station," he said to Larry. "It can't get through a cordon like that. I hope you're in good shooting form."

Larry's mousy little face lit up in a merry grin. "Never better," he said. "Women and children are acting as beaters, right?"

"Nat Phelps is seeing to that," said Dr. Bailey. "I've saved you the most likely post. Come and see."

The two of them went squelching out through the gate again, leaving me standing with Elaine, feeling sick. Elaine didn't look too happy, either. But she went striding away to give someone orders, and I just stood there.

It was a lovely spring day, that was the worst of it. The sun came up and up, bright and mild and warm, as people kept arriving. Everyone was there. I saw Mr. A. C. Taylor the druggist, hurrying across the field with a gun, and the men in boots from the boats, the postman, the milkman, and the booted porter from the station. They all had guns. Benita Wallins was handing out paper cups of tea from the back of an old van. Adele Taylor and Corinne West were strolling about in expensive trousers and pretty anoraks. I saw most of the Mrs. Urs sooner or later, including Phyllis Forbes, who came marshaling a crowd of orphans through the gate. One of the clone boys had his arm in a very white sling. There were crowds of other people, too, all trampling the dandelions in the grass of the field. Almost the only people I *didn't* see were Dad and Zenobia Bailey.

I wondered resentfully why they kept Dad away. I still do.

Mr. Phelps drove in through the gate in a little high

black car with an open top. He parpled the horn noisily and began shouting orders before he had stopped the car.

"All women and children assemble by me. Come on. No slacking."

Nobody seemed to take much notice of the orders, but everybody slowly did seem to get more businesslike. Men ran or walked into the distance to make a long line that seemed to stretch right up to Cranbury Head. A lot of them went out the gate, like Larry and Dr. Bailey, and I supposed they were making a line the other way, right up to the orphanage and maybe beyond that.

Mr. Phelps was marching up and down shouting things like, "Everyone got their lunch packs? The lunch pack of Notre Dame—ha, ha! Come on, get organized. We want to catch this beastie napping!"

I think it was Elaine who did the organizing. With a white contemptuous look at Mr. Phelps every so often, she got the orphans into two Land Rovers and a van, and all the other females into a procession of smaller cars. I ended up sitting beside Hester Bailey in her Land Rover full of orphans. She kept turning to me and smiling as she drove and saying sensible things like, "You mustn't be scared. Safety in numbers. We have to drive it down on the guns, you know."

I thought resentfully of Dad and her two-foot-high daughter Zenobia. I said, "Why do they have to shoot it?"

"It's dangerous, dear," Hester Bailey said briskly.

"Possibly even rabid."

We drove right up into the hills, into a high field above the goblin woods. We all piled out with our lunch packs, and my heart was banging in my throat. I looked at the fields and hills and farms stretching inland behind us, and I hoped Chris had had the sense to get out into those and stay there.

Mr. Phelps made us a Jerry-is-here speech then. I couldn't terribly listen. It was all about the wings doubling back on the main body and our *cordon sanitaire* and choosing the spot for the engagement and avoiding cross fire. I think he meant that men with guns were going to be on the hills on either side of Cranbury Bay. They were going to close in, and we were all going to fill in the middle. Then he began passing out sticks, thick ones, from the backseat of his car and telling us very carefully what we were to do.

I thought, Chris can easily get past a line of orphans with sticks.

But then a tractor came chugging up across the high field, towing a cart full of more men with guns. "Ah, here comes the farm contingent," said Mr. Phelps. He was delighted. "My reinforcements. One armed man to every ten beaters. That will make absolutely sure the brute can't double back."

The men with guns had caps and ferrety faces. You couldn't tell whether they were young or old. They all came leaping down from the cart in a businesslike way, but there was a sort of swing to their movements that showed they were as pleased as Larry had been at the thought of shooting a real wild animal. "It's in there," they said. "Seen it this morning."

Then we were ready to go at last. While we were milling about, being shared out between the farm men, someone took hold of my shoulder in a policeman's grip. I whirled round. It was Elaine. She was gray-white.

"I hope you warned him," she said in a growling whisper. "He's not going to escape this in a hurry."

I stared up at her, twisted round. She knew. She must have heard Chris howl in the garden that night. "Yes, I did," I said.

"Good," she said. "I wouldn't have let you get away with it for anyone else." She let go of me and strode off to go with Benita Wallins.

"Everybody enter the woods. *Now*!" bellowed Mr. Phelps.

We all walked slowly downward among the twisted trees. Most people swished their sticks and shouted. I didn't. I wanted to sneak away, but there was always at least one man with a gun tramping slowly down behind me, and I was never out of sight of Selma Tidmarsh on my right or the orphan with the sling on my left. Every so often Mr. Phelps came bounding past behind us, calling, "Ten feet apart, now. Keep that line straight there!"

You could tell he was loving every moment. I wanted to shout to him that he had no business to be hunting Chris, who had only tried to help him, but I could see it would do no good.

We went on down, going sideways and back round twisted tree trunks, bending under twisty branches loaded with yellow-green buds, stumbling on logs and cracking twigs. At first it was hot. There were midges out, circling in slants of misty sunshine. I remember us tramping through a band of those bright yellow shiny flowers and then across spindly white windflowers. We stamped on toadstools and crunched down acres of crusty gray-green moss stuff. The orphan on my left took his arm out of the white sling in order to hold on to branches in the steep bits.

We disturbed all the birds and lots of animals. The first time the first rabbit sprang up and pelted away downhill my insides gave a sick surge, even though I could see it was small. Some of the farm men took pot-shots at the things we disturbed. The first time the first bang came echoing along the trees, the wood went kind of gray round me and swung about. But I got used to it and just felt dull.

"Only a rabbit. Keep on, keep on!" Mr. Phelps would shout, pelting past. Sometimes messages to stop were passed down the line, when people got behind or too far in front. Selma Tidmarsh and the orphan fetched things out of their lunch bags and ate them when this happened. I couldn't. I fetched out a dry-looking sandwich the first time and had to throw it away. During one stoppage, when Selma Tidmarsh was talking to the person on the other side of her, I went sideways over to the orphan.

"Is your arm very bad?" I said.

His sling was hanging round his neck. He looked at his right arm, then his left, and finally, in a puzzled way, he rolled up his left sleeve. There was nothing wrong with his arm at all. He looked surprised.

An illusion, like the car, I thought. "Don't worry. Just checking," I said, and moved back to my place.

On down we went. The sun slanted away to the twisted top of the trees. Dampness came up round our legs, smelling of leaves and earth and mushrooms. By this time I was kind of dulled to the shouts and calls and occasional bangs. When there were three loud bangs and a lot of shouting over to my left, I took no notice at first.

Then Mr. Phelps sped past yelling, "Keep the line, keep the line. We've got it, but we don't want it doubling back!"

Everything went suddenly tense. There was a briskness to the way everyone walked down. Before long, I could tell there really was quite a large animal down ahead of us. There was swishing and twigs snapping. Once I caught sight of a heavy gray shadow as something fled desperately along the hill, trying to find a way round the line. Oh, Chris! I thought. Chris, I warned you!

Down we went. Quite suddenly we were at the edge of the woods looking over a field of new corn where the sun was going down misty pink, and birds we had disturbed were going round and round in the sky, black birds from the woods and white birds from the sea, cawing and crying. Mr. Phelps was cawing and crying instructions, but I don't remember what they were. I only remember the line of men facing us on the other side of the field. Some were kneeling, some standing. I think some were even lying down, but they all had guns aimed at the wood.

And I remember the gray dog-shaped thing that ran out from the trees way over to the left of me. It stopped when it saw the men, turned back to the wood, realized it couldn't, and began to run sideways along the field in a terrified low snaking dash. The guns began going off. *Bang* and *bang.* White smoke came in blots in the blue air. And the wolf sprang into the air, twisted two ways at once. Then it fell down with its legs threshing.

There was a great shout from the other side of the field. "*Bull's-eye.* I *got* her!" I could see Larry Mr. Elaine dancing about there, waving his gun over his head, as I began to run toward the wolf. It had stopped moving before I got halfway. Mr. Phelps was running after me, roaring to me to keep back. Out of the corner of my eye

I could see the tall black shape of Elaine running, too. But I took no notice and ran until I came to the wolf, spread out on its side with its eyes staring.

It was huge, much bigger than I expected, and much, much thinner. I stared stupidly at the stiff arch of its stomach and the two rows of little nipples on it. I stared at its jaws, open in a snarl, and the pink foam on its gray, broken teeth. I thought, I don't *believe* it! It's not Chris, after all!

"Aha! Old she-wolf!" Mr. Phelps said, rubbing his hands together.

The men with the guns were all shaking hands and shouting congratulations to Larry and one another. Someone was coming trotting along the hedge with mugs of beer for them.

"Well, that's a relief," Elaine said behind me. She had her two-line smile. "Come on. I'll drive you home."

We didn't say anything to each other the whole way. I felt unreal, as if the top of my head had come off and let my brains out. I couldn't stop smiling. Elaine stopped the car outside Aunt Maria's garden gate and marched me in through the kitchen. Aunt Maria and Mum were in the dining room. When she saw us, Aunt Maria hoisted herself eagerly forward on her sticks.

"Well, dear? Did they get him?"

"They shot an old she-wolf," Elaine said.

Aunt Maria fell back into her chair and stared. "Naomi," she said, in a feeble gasping voice. "Not my Naomi!"

"Well, you told them to shoot a wolf," Elaine said, and she turned on the heel of her green boot and marched out of the house again. I heard her slam the back door through the noise Aunt Maria was making.

She was screaming by then, in a way that made Mum and me feel sick. "Naomi! Oh, Naomi!" she yelled.

"But Mig's *here*!" Mum kept saying. "Do stop, Auntie!"

We couldn't get her to stop, whatever we said. For once in my life I was glad when the doorbell rang and the Mrs. Urs began trooping in. "Oh, the poor dear!" they said when they heard the screaming, and they ran up the hall in their muddy boots. "You can't blame the men," Adele Taylor said to me as she passed me. "They only did as they were told."

There was such a crowd in the dining room, and still such a noise from Aunt Maria, that Mum and I were trying to back out when Zoe Green pushed the front door open and stood scraping the mud off her boots on the doormat. She was wrapped in an old knitted blanket. She was the only one who cleaned her boots. She stared at us and arched her head to the noise. "Taking on, izs zshe?" she said. Mum nodded, even though it was obvious. Zoe Green nodded back in her mad way and shuffled up the hall, sort of sidling toward us. "Good," she whispered. "The men meandt to do it, too!" I had to wipe spit off me.

While I did, Zoe Green banged the dining-room door open and shouted out, "Oh, poor dhear! Ndow you know how I feel!"

Aunt Maria screamed back, "Curse you, Zoe Green! I *curse* you, you uncharitable woman!"

"Now, now, now, dear!" everyone else said. Mum and I went into the living room to get away.

"Was it very awful, love?" Mum asked.

"Yes," I said. "I thought it was Chris at first. But I think Zoe Green was right. I heard Larry shout 'I got her!' when he was much too far away to see."

Mum gave me a soothing, bewildered smile and picked up her pea green knitting. "I shall be glad to leave this place," she said. That made me feel almost hopeful.

eLeVEn

Chris didn't turn up that night. I'm sure he was scared to. And I didn't wake up and Lavinia never moved from Mum's neck the whole night. In the morning, the food I had put out was still there. I gave a lot of it to Lavinia, and I felt very lonely.

Aunt Maria was still in a terrible state. Her face was white and baggy. She kept grabbing me with her shaky old hand and saying, "Dear little Naomi. You make it up to me, don't you, dear?"

I didn't know what she was on about, so I just said, "I suppose so," and got free as soon as I could each time.

Then she wanted me to come to church with her. Luckily by then I really hadn't any clothes that weren't muddy. Mum said I was to stay behind. I was glad. It wasn't just that Aunt Maria going to church is a sham—and it isn't quite a sham, or at least it's a muddled sham, because I can see Aunt Maria really believes she is good and charitable and religious. The important thing was that I had to see Miss Phelps. Secretly, if possible. I knew I had to talk to someone neutral who understood.

Larry came along with the wheelchair. "Elaine's got a headache," he said. He still looked twice as jolly as I've ever seen him before, almost jaunty. He and Mum loaded Aunt Maria and her dead fox into the chair, and they set off.

I was halfway across the kitchen on my way out when the back door opened. Elaine stood there. "Oh, no, you don't," she said. "I'll let you feed him, but that's all. Go back inside and sit down."

She marched me into the living room and made me sit on Aunt Maria's roped sofa. She sat opposite in my usual chair, where she fetched a little white piece of embroidery out of her pocket and a thimble and scissors, and sat with her legs neatly together sewing. It looked very unsuitable. She kept snipping tiny holes and embroidering round them.

"What are you doing that for?" I said.

"I haven't come to talk," Elaine said. "Get on with something of your own."

I couldn't get on with writing. Aunt Maria doesn't bother to look at what I'm doing, but I knew Elaine would. I knew I was trapped for the morning with nothing to do, so I didn't care what I said. "Who was that she-wolf?" I said. "Aunt Maria's daughter?"

Elaine didn't answer, but I knew I was right.

"Why do you like Chris so much?" I said.

"I like all men," Elaine said. I could see a big grin on her face, even though she bent over her sewing to hide it. "I like making them like me. Chris likes me."

"Even Mr. Phelps?" I said.

Elaine did her clock-strike laugh. "Nat Phelps is scared of me, because he knows I'll get him in the end," she said.

"That's greedy," I said. "You've got Larry."

"Yes," said Elaine, and stopped smiling. "I've got Larry."

"It's your fault he's so boring. You've made him that way," I said.

She put her head up and positively glared at me for that. "Shut up," she said.

I didn't care. I knew she hated me, anyway. "Did you get Antony Green, too?" I said.

Elaine's head was still back and the way her fanatical eyes gazed at me made me wish I hadn't asked. But she bent back over her sewing and said calmly, "Before my time, that one. But I've heard he wasn't easy to deal with."

"Why?" I said.

"Why—y—y?" Elaine whined, imitating me. "Lord, aren't children boring! Because, they tell me, the silly innocent refused to believe other people were different from himself."

"What's wrong with that?" I cried.

"Nothing, provided you're the same as other people to start with," said Elaine. "*I've* no wish to be treated in the same way as Larry, thank you."

I didn't understand. I began to ask, but she snapped, "I *told* you I didn't come to talk. One more word and I'll *make* you shut up. Do you think I can't?"

I didn't think she couldn't, so I stopped talking. The morning dragged on for several years, until Larry and Mum hoisted Aunt Maria back into the hall. Elaine gave me a grim look and left when she heard them opening the front door.

So I had to wait until the afternoon, when I knew everyone would be sitting behind lace curtains spying on me. But it wasn't as bad as that, because Aunt Maria gave Mum the afternoon off.

"Go and get some air, dears," she said to us both. "I shall be quite all right."

I think she wanted to talk about the dead wolf without us hearing.

It was another nice warm spring day, but I was careful to take my anorak. Mum and I walked past the twitching lace curtains and then down onto the sand at the near end of the promenade. I took us over to a huddle of round rocks and got Mum arranged sitting on one. Then I took my anorak off and shaped it over one of the small round rocks, so that if anyone looked from the promenade it might just seem like a smaller person, sitting humped up beside Mum. Then I sat on the sand out of sight of the houses and said, "Mum, can you humor me for a while? Can you sit here and pretend to be talking to this rock disguised as me?"

"I suppose so," Mum said. "People do watch and gossip, don't they? How long is it supposed to be for?"

"I may be away two hours," I said. "Do you think you'll be all right?"

"I wish you'd warned me, Miggie. I'd have brought my knitting," Mum said. Then she laughed and stretched her arms up and out. "I'll be fine! Don't look so worried. There's nothing I want more than just to sit in peace for a couple of hours. Aunt Maria's worn me to a frazzle. If I get bored, I'll collect shells."

I got up into a crouch, ready to dash to cover under the rocks at the end of the promenade. Before I went, I tried to remind Mum of Chris again. "Don't you think it's funny without Chris?" I said.

"Yes, I do," Mum said. "I keep wishing we hadn't left him in London."

So it's worked round to that now, I thought, as I ran for the rocks, and then started up the steep little stairs I had seen Mr. Phelps using. She thinks she left Chris behind. That probably gave me courage to go on. It was such a lovely calm day, with the light all sideways and golden, and the sea in flat sparkles, that I'd been very tempted to sit beside Mum and hope things would turn out all right. But it's no good thinking happy endings just happen.

This end of the bay was rocks, not proper cliffs, and people's garden walls backed onto the sea. I was fairly sure one of the gardens was the Phelps's, but not quite sure. I walked along, counting the gardens carefully and looking for Phelpsish signs, until Mum was out of sight somewhere below and I was sure I'd gone too far. I thought I'd better go on to the end of the walls and come carefully back. And I'd gone on some way more, when I noticed that the path ahead stopped being so well trodden. I looked at the garden door beside the last trodden piece. It was painted plain dark blue. It didn't look particularly Phelpsish, but I tried the latch, anyway, and it opened.

The garden inside was marvelous. It was all little paths made of shells and white stones, and there was a model windmill in the middle. In between the paths were flower beds full of daffodils and blue hyacinths. Silver bells and cockleshells, I thought, tiptoeing up the straightest path to the house. It took me some time to dare to ring the little silver bell hanging by the blue back door, in case it was somebody else's garden entirely.

Or suppose it's a Mrs. Ur! I thought, and nearly ran away when I heard someone shooting a bolt back inside the door.

The door slammed open and Mr. Phelps stood there in his dressing gown. He glared at me and then turned to glare back over his shoulder. "You've won that bet, blast you!" he shouted. "It's the girl."

"Tell her to come in, Nathaniel, please," Miss Phelps's clear little voice called out.

Mr. Phelps jerked his head at me and stood aside to let me in. When I went in, there was the tiny shape of Miss Phelps, working her way down the passage toward me.

"Good afternoon," she said. Then she fell over again. This time she just went over straight forward, the way you do when you're playing at falling down on your bed. Only she went *smack* on the floor.

I dived to help her. Mr. Phelps said, "I wish you wouldn't keep doing that," and shut the back door. Then he stepped over me and Miss Phelps and stalked away down the passage into one of the rooms there. Just like Dad when Mum fell downstairs, I thought, kneeling in the nearly dark hallway.

"I prefer to lie here awhile," Miss Phelps said. "I heard a crack this time, and I'd like to wait and see what it was. Open that door behind you so that we can have a little light. We can talk here as well as anywhere." When I had opened the door, revealing Miss Phelps lying on her front with her chin on her arms and her gnomelike glasses on her nose, and looking very polite, somehow, she said, "Don't be too hard on my brother. He does all the cooking and most of the housework these days, you know. And we both hold the view that help is not needed unless it's asked for. Now what did you want?"

"I want help," I said. "Please. I know you're neutral. But I'm not. You know Chris is a wolf now, don't you? Is Lavinia a cat?"

"Very probably," said Miss Phelps. "She was always good at animals. But she's good at a fair number of other things, too. I hope you were careful coming here."

"I was," I said. "Is Antony Green's ghost the only one who can turn Chris back? Or will the green box do it?"

"Um," said Miss Phelps. "When I told you nobody talks about that person, I meant it. She makes sure of that. I think it's a painful subject to her, because her Naomi somehow met the same fate as your Chris over it. We'll have to ask my brother about that and the green box. Talk about something else until I'm ready to get up."

"The clones—I mean the orphans—then," I said. "Why are they the only children in the place?"

"Because they *are* the children in the place, of course," said Miss Phelps. "She wanted the next generation of adults properly trained. But don't imagine that's the only time that's been tried. Some of the holders of the green box went even further in the past and tried to breed a whole race of folk."

"Some of the orphans are black, though," I said.

"They still divide into male and female whatever their color," said Miss Phelps. "They imported a few. She had to get the council to pay somehow. But, as I told her, the experiment has always failed in the past, and it's bound to fail now, since she hasn't got the proper person to take over when she goes. Elaine won't do. The power goes with the person."

"Is that what you said?" I asked. "To annoy her so?"

"No. I also told her her ways were quite out of date," Miss Phelps said briskly. "Is there anything else before I start getting up?"

"About Dad," I said. "Why are they pretending he is dead?"

"You *have* found out a great deal," Miss Phelps said. She began to struggle slowly to her hands and knees, panting out, "Stupid melodrama, if you ask me. Clean break with the outside, I suppose. They must think he can use the green box. Not many people can touch it, you know. But these are men's affairs. Just wait till I get up. . . ."

I hauled her up to her large swollen feet. She looked very surprised. "*Is* something broken?" I said.

"Time will tell," she said. "Nathaniel is in the front room, I believe."

I took hold of her arm and made sure we got there. Mr. Phelps was stretched out on the sofa where Chris and I had sat, fast asleep, snoring gobbling snores that quivered his thin purple throat. I suppose he was tired after the hunt, and after cooking their Sunday lunch. I could smell the lunch in the passage. It seemed a shame to wake him up.

But Miss Phelps was quite ruthless. She shuffled over to him, still hanging on to me, and gave him a straight-fingered jab in the middle of his dressing gown. It made him toss his legs in the air with a howl. "Nathaniel, you are not to take refuge in sleep," she said. "You know she was bound to want to ask you things. Come, sit up and be civil."

Mr. Phelps sat up and smoothed his thin gray hair. He looked angry and dignified.

Miss Phelps said, "You are not to be afraid of him, Margaret. He needs you as much as you need him. If you will help me to my chair while he adjusts to this, we shall begin our conference." So I helped her to her special chair, where she climbed up like a small monkey, and then said, "Well, Nathaniel? Speak to her of your green man. You know I can't."

"Antony Green," said Mr. Phelps. "But you know as well as I do that we don't *know* what happened to him. Except that now we got the she-wolf, there is a chance things will get better." He smiled, very satisfied. "She very seldom makes a mistake of an order like that."

"She's getting old," said Miss Phelps from her chair.

"And the men's time will come again," Mr. Phelps said, nodding. "But we need someone to handle the green box for us first." He looked fanatically at me. "It's as old as time, that. As old as this country. You know what you did, don't you, girl? You drained it half away. I still had hopes that your brother might be our next handler, and then he gets himself turned wolf."

"Tell me how to turn him back again," I said. Mr. Phelps did frighten me, in spite of what Miss Phelps said. "Can Antony Green's ghost do it?"

"Ghost?" said Mr. Phelps. "The man's not dead."

"Speak to him of the ghost," Miss Phelps said, like a chairperson.

So I told Mr. Phelps of the three times I saw Antony Green. He planted his mauve hands on his thin knees and leaned forward, saying, "And what else? You were sure he could speak? Describe that light in the room. Accurately, mind." And when I had done my best, he turned to Miss Phelps. They looked at each other questioningly.

"A ghost," Miss Phelps said, "to my certain knowledge, performs the same, or almost the same, actions every time it manifests. This one did varied things."

"And seemed only aware of young Chris at first," said Mr. Phelps, hands on knees, stiffly thinking.

"But transferred his attention to Margaret later," Miss Phelps reminded him. "And the light, Nathaniel."

"Yes, the light is the clincher," murmured Mr. Phelps.

"Your ghost," Miss Phelps said to me, "is not a ghost in our opinion. It is a personal projection, a sending if you like, in which a living person throws some part of himself from one place to another. The light will be caused by the force used by the sender changing the particles of air to form the image. Such images can speak."

"Yes, I always thought Antony had something of his own beside what the box gave him," said Mr. Phelps. "You must get him to speak, girl. Make him tell you where he is, really. We can fetch him back then. Do that. It's the only chance your brother has."

"But he won't *speak*!" I wailed. I didn't mean to cry, but I did. Great tears ran beside my nose and I sobbed out, "And the worst of it is, I can't get Mum to notice Chris isn't there! First she thought he was always just out of sight, and now she thinks we left him behind in London."

Mr. Phelps was disgusted with me. "Women's wiles!" he said. "Stop blubbering. Your mother's not that important."

"Don't be unfeeling, Nathaniel," Miss Phelps said across the room. "The child is upset. She can do with any help she can get. An injunction has clearly been laid on her mother. Can you think of any way she can break it?"

"I don't deal with women," said Mr. Phelps.

"Then treat it as a purely intellectual problem," said Miss Phelps.

We all sat for a bit. Mr. Phelps folded his arms and seemed angry. But after a while he began saying, "Let's see. She called her mother's attention to her brother's absence. Didn't you, girl? And that seems to have reinforced the injunction, so the mother now believes the boy is elsewhere entirely. Tell me the various ways you told her."

I wiped my nose on my only tattered Kleenex and told him.

He said at each thing, "Hm, so that idea won't work. . . ." "I don't know," he said at last. "They usually can be broken, but this one seems uncommonly cunningly set up. I wonder why."

"Mrs. Laker is extremely useful in the house," Miss Phelps said drily. "She's a far better factotum than Lavinia ever was."

Then we all sat about again while Mr. Phelps shook his head. "You have to get her to see it some way that doesn't have direct bearing on Chris," he said. "That's all I can say."

Miss Phelps said, thinking, too, "Suppose you try showing her the ghost, if he comes again. Or has she seen it already?"

"No," I said. "Come to think of it, I don't think she's ever been in Chris's room! Oh, thanks. I'll try that."

"But don't build too much on it," said Miss Phelps. "Now I think you should be going before somebody notices you're not where you should be."

Mr. Phelps showed me out through the garden, acting very courtly now, though the wind blew his dressing gown about. I said, "I do think this is a lovely garden." He was ever so pleased. It turned out that he'd done all the paths with shells himself. I suppose I should have tried to flatter him before. But I really don't like managing people by those rules. Still, Mr. Phelps does go by those rules himself, and perhaps he expected it.

Mum was beginning to shiver in the evening wind, collecting shells, but she was all right. "Mum, will you humor me again?" I asked.

"I might. Unless it means sitting on the beach two hours more," she said. "What?"

"I'll tell you later tonight," I said. "Promise?"

"Promise," she said.

twelve

"THE STORY OF THE TWIN PRINCESSES"

BY N. M. LAKER

Just look what Aunt Maria wrote on the title page of my old story!

Dear Naomi,

I see from the last few pages of your other writing that Elaine is right. I have been much too trusting. You should not have gone to see the Phelpses, child. They are petty people who do not understand as you and I do, but they can only sow poison—that is the extent of their malice, and I know no real harm is done.

I give you this story instead and suggest

you finish it while you meditate on how deeply you have hurt me.

Your loving,
Aunt Maria

In other words, disaster has struck. I am having to write the rest of this on the blank pages I left in "The Twin Princesses." How lucky I did. The paper is furry and smells of mildew, and I am locked in. But at least I am still in human shape. And Aunt Maria doesn't know all the other things that happened before Elaine stole my biography. It is lucky I didn't have time to write any more.

I did hope Chris would come that night after I went to the Phelpses, but he didn't. He seems to have disappeared entirely. I keep being afraid he's been run over or shot by farmers inland.

Anyway, as soon as Aunt Maria started snoring that night, I whispered to Mum, "Mum, you promised you'd humor me."

Poor Mum. She was terribly tired. She said she'd hoped I'd forgotten, but she got out of bed, sighing, and said what did I want.

"Put your coat on and come down and sit with me in Chris's room," I said.

She was so sleepy she must have forgotten she thought Chris was in London. But she made a fuss because nothing would possess Lavinia to come down with us. I think the injunction must have been working that way. Lavinia scratched us both and bolted. "Oh, *leave* her!" I whispered angrily.

"What kind of lever, dear?" Aunt Maria called instantly.

"I said Mig has a slight *fever,* Auntie," Mum called, coming to my rescue. "We're going downstairs to see what we can do for it. You go to sleep."

"Call Dr. Bailey!" Aunt Maria said sleepily.

"In the morning," Mum called soothingly.

It worked. Aunt Maria was snoring again as we went into Chris's room. Mum held her candle up and looked round it in a bewildered way. "Where's Chris?" she said. I had hopes for a moment, until she said, "Oh, downstairs eating tomorrow's lunch again, obviously. Look at the way he leaves his bed. What am I to humor *you* in, Mig?"

"By sitting here and waiting for Chris," I said. "There's something I want to discuss with you both."

Mum sat on Chris's bed. She yawned, then shivered. "Must the window be open?"

"Yes," I said. "That's important." I was still hoping Chris would jump through it then. It is fortunate Mum is so very saintly and obliging. She looked resigned. She pulled Chris's covers round both our shoulders and we sat leaning our backs against the wall, watching the little pointed candle flame quiver on the end of the candle.

"What are we waiting for?" Mum asked, giving a bit of a jump. It was much later. I could tell because the candle had burnt much further down, spilling a long transparent waterfall of wax down one side.

"Don John of Austria," I said. "I hope."

Mum sort of laughed. "Am I still humoring you?" she asked hopefully.

I said, "Yes," and we both went to sleep again.

I had the dream again. It is worse each time you have it, because as soon as it starts you know what you're in for. Years and years of being shut inside the ground, desperate useless rages and frantic fighting to get out. It's horrible the way feet run over the top of you, too. I burst out of it finally and looked up at the ghost in the strange dim light. The candle was out. He had one eyebrow up and was looking at me expectantly.

"I'm working on it," I told him. "This time I brought . . . " I looked round and realized that Mum was fast asleep. She looked terribly peaceful and pretty with the light shining on her rounded forehead and her little nose, and none of her wrinkles showing.

I dug my elbow into her and she leaped up with her hands to her head, crying out, "Oh, *Lord,* I was having a horrible dream!" She saw the ghost, and he saw her. They both looked thoroughly amazed. "Who . . . who?" said Mum.

"The ghost," I said. "At least, he's not. He's alive. This

is his projection . . . er . . . sending from wherever he is."

The ghost looked at me then. There was real hope in his face.

"Who *is* he?" said Mum.

"He's called Antony Green," I said.

The ghost gave us both a little bow at that. His mane of hair flopped. And he turned to me expectantly.

"Mr. Phelps says you *must* talk," I said. "He can let you out if he knows where you are."

"Yes, *do* you talk?" Mum said.

He looked from one to the other of us and began smiling his long smile.

"Oh, *what* a smile!" Mum said.

"Yes, but be careful," I said. "He usually goes away after that. It's a twisting-you-round-his-finger smile like Chris does."

"Yes, I *see,*" Mum said. "Poor man, he's not quite all here, is he? No, wait a minute," she said. The ghost was starting to go. I could see books through him. Mum jumped off Chris's bed and stumbled toward the ghost, all mixed up in Chris's covers. He backed away from her, until he really was in the bookshelf, among all the books there. "Don't go yet," Mum said. "Let me look at you. Stand still . . . er . . . Antony Green."

He stayed where he was, staring at Mum with a hurt, inquiring sort of look on his crooked face. It really was strange. Mum stood, bending a bit forward, peering at him embedded in the bookshelf.

"I think you've got yourself wrong," was the first thing Mum said after a while. "Nobody looks quite this odd. But you're putting out your own idea of yourself, aren't you? I suppose it's quite a privilege to see it." Then she stared a while longer and said, "That dream—you brought that dream, didn't you? Is that where you are, how you feel? It *is*, isn't it?" The ghost was nodding slowly. "And you're alive? Mig says you're alive," Mum said. The ghost was still nodding. Mum looked angrily over her shoulder at me. "Mig, why didn't you explain at *once*? As soon as you met him. We could have got him out weeks ago!" And she rounded on the ghost again. "You have to tell me where you are," she said, "and we'll come and get you. Can you please explain exactly where you are?"

The ghost put up his shoulders and spread his hands out. I thought he meant he couldn't say, but Mum nodded and said, "I see. And how do we find that out?" The ghost raised a shadowy hand and pointed, first away somewhere, then more or less at me. "I *think* I see," Mum said. The ghost was fading all the time now. She said, "I think that's everything. You can let go now. I'll be with you as soon as we can."

The ghost was a mere blur by then. I could only see his strange crooked face. "Mum!" I said. "Make him wait!" But he vanished while I was saying it. "We never asked him about Chris!" I wailed in the dark.

"He couldn't stay, Mig. Couldn't you see?" Mum said. "It took him a tremendous effort to be here at all." She stumbled about in the dark. "Where's the candle? What made it go out?"

"He always puts it out," I said. I found the matches and her hand and put the two together. "There was something urgent I needed him to do," I said.

"There can't be anything more urgent than he is himself," Mum said, lighting the candle. She had fierce wrinkles in her forehead. "You can't find someone who's buried alive and then *ask* them things!" she said. "Goodness, Mig, surely you can see that." Then she sat down with her face in her hands. "Now let me think a minute. My head's in rather a whirl!"

I let her think. Now she put it that way, I was very ashamed at not seeing for myself the trouble Antony Green was in. And I sighed. If I couldn't ask him to help about Chris, there was no Don John of Austria after all, and what was I to do?

This time it was Mum's elbow that dug into *me.* "Mig, wake up. I've just realized I haven't seen Chris for nearly a week. Where *is* he?"

Seeing the ghost had worked, after all. I flung my arms round her and babbled explanations. She wouldn't believe me at first. I thrust the blankets at her. "Smell!" I said. "Wolf." I offered to get my biography as proof, but that wouldn't do. She seems to think I always write fiction. So I said, "You believe Antony Green is a ghost buried alive. Why not this about Chris, too?"

That did it. Mum said, "But that means that yesterday, when they were hunting the wolf—*Mig*! They didn't *shoot* Chris?"

"No. It was another wolf, a she-wolf," I said. "Aunt Maria meant them to shoot Chris, though."

Mum was angry. Oh, she was angry. The worm turned all right in the middle of that night. "And to think I've been waiting hand and foot on that—that *evil* old woman!" she said. She raged. She called everyone names I'd never heard before. "Well-done, Chris, with her evil bloomers!" she said. "Mig, I thought he was a dog. I'm glad I let him out of the house. Now I wonder . . . what's the soonest we can go back and talk to your Miss Phelps? She'll be asleep now. We'd better go first thing in the morning."

"Before you do," I said. "There's another thing. Dad's alive. I talked to him."

"He was always much too enmeshed in this horrid little dump," Mum said. "No wonder, really. Tell." So I did. She said, "He does pick 'em. Zenobia Bailey's almost as bad a name as Verena Bland. Poor Greg. Does he want out, Mig, or is he quite happy?"

"Happy," I said. "Not quite happy."

"That'll have to do," Mum said. We went back to bed

then or, as Mum said, Aunt Maria would be banging for breakfast before either of us had got to sleep. Lavinia was awfully pleased to see us. She must have thought the ghost had eaten us, silly thing.

In the morning, I could hardly see for yawning, but Mum swiftly buttoned and hooked Aunt Maria into her clothes. "You're coming down for breakfast today," she said.

"I know, dear," said Aunt Maria. "Elaine's coming to take me out at ten. Are you coming with us?"

That rather took the wind out of Mum's sails, but she said, "No, Mig and I are going out ourselves. I want that quite clear. This *is* our Easter holiday, you know."

"Of course, dear. So good of you to spend it with me—quite devoted," said Aunt Maria. Mum made exasperated faces at me over Aunt Maria's head. And I made faces back to leave it at that.

Elaine gave me several forbidding looks while she was wheeling Aunt Maria down the hall, but I didn't think about it much. I just wanted them to go. As soon as they had, I said to Mum, "We have to go up that path behind the gardens."

"Why have we?" she said. "I intend simply to walk across the street and knock on the door. No one can stop us."

"They can turn us into things afterward," I said.

"Yes, that is frightening," Mum agreed. "But I feel

like a demonstration, Mig. Chris made his. You've been writing down exactly what you think—"

"Yes, but that was sneaky," I said. "I didn't dare say it."

"Well, I dare you to cross the road with me now," Mum said.

And we did. I was terrified. The road seemed a mile wide, with telescopes trained on it from behind every lacy window, but nobody did anything to stop us. And Mr. Phelps opened the door as we reached it.

"Good day to you, ma'am," he said. "We were expecting you. My sister's in here." He brought us into the room where Miss Phelps sat like a gnome in her high chair. They were so much expecting us that there were four cups of coffee waiting on the table and a plate of ginger cookies.

Mum went and shook hands with Miss Phelps, and we were all awfully polite for quite a while. Then Mum said, "About Antony Green—" and both Phelpses leaned forward until Miss Phelps nearly fell out of her chair. Mum said, "I think one or other of you might have told someone he's buried alive! How long has he been missing?"

"Twenty years," said Miss Phelps. Mum began to steam at the ears. Miss Phelps held up a little monkey paw to stop her. "I assure you neither of us knew what had become of him," she said, "until Margaret described him yesterday."

"Christian didn't mention the dreams," Mr. Phelps said. "Understandable."

"You mean, how like a boy to cover up nasty emotions," Miss Phelps said. "We have been trying to find out about the person you're concerned about for twenty years. Neither of us liked to see the women ruling unchecked."

"Oh, dear," said Mum. "I'd hoped—You see, he told me last night that he had to be let out by the same person who buried him."

"*Did* he?" I said. "I didn't hear him say a word."

"It was very faint," Mum said. "You could only hear if you concentrated hard."

"Oh," I said. "It did sound rather like a telephone conversation. All I heard was you. But what do we do? We don't even know where he is, let alone who put him there."

"I know where," said Mum. "It was in the dream. It's a kind of mound with bushes growing on it, and people keep running across it all the time."

"*Oh!*" all three of the rest of us cried out. "Just by the Greens' old house," said Miss Phelps. "It's an orphanage now, but I used to play on that mound as a child."

I found I was looking at Mr. Phelps. We both felt stupid. "Chris knew," I said. "Didn't he even tell *you*?"

"Er . . . mm. He may not have known when I spoke to him," said Mr. Phelps. "The question now is, who put him there?" He looked across at Miss Phelps.

"Time travel, I think," she said briskly. "Or do either of you get travel-sick? Nathaniel finds he can only travel as an animal, but probably that is just as well. A cat or a dog is never much noticed and never, of course, in the wrong clothes."

Mum and I sort of gooped at one another.

"We do know almost the exact day and hour Antony disappeared, ma'am," Mr. Phelps said. "But we never narrowed down the place. We thought it must be somewhere in Loup Woods. His coat was found there, you know. In fact, I was sure it was the woods, though I've been over nearly every inch of them now in some form or other."

Mum went on staring.

"Or maybe they don't trust us, Nathaniel," said Miss Phelps. "This was why I suggested Nathaniel should go with you. I would offer myself, only I fear I would make a very crippled cat and slow you down dreadfully. You *have* offered to go, haven't you, Nathaniel?"

"Naturally," said Mr. Phelps, though he didn't look as if he liked the idea. "As Antony Green's chief lieutenant, this concerns me, too."

"It's just," I said, "that Mum and I aren't used to . . . time travel and so forth."

"It's the way you both speak—so matter-of-factly," Mum said, and added warily, "You did say cats, did you?"

"A demonstration, ma'am," said Mr. Phelps. He stood up and slipped off his dressing gown. While it was still in the air as he threw it to the sofa, he was not there. But there was a bundle of clothes on the floor where he had been, and a tabby cat with slightly fanatical eyes was sitting on them looking at us.

"Quite painless, you see," said Miss Phelps. And she called out, "Nathaniel, I may as well send you off now. No time like the present." She turned to Mum. "I believe that is a joke. Will you go next?"

I delayed things a bit. I did so love being a cat. It was a bit puzzling at first, when I climbed out of my clothes, because my muscles moved my light little body twice as easily as I expected. I shot forward into the middle of the floor and landed with my legs spread out in all directions. I could hear Miss Phelps laughing somewhere very high up. The way I heard things was different. The way I saw things was *very* different. I blinked and blinked until I got used to my magnifying cat-eyes, which showed me all sorts of interesting bits of fluff right in the distance in the dark places under the sofa. I smelled the fluff. Seeing and smelling were mixed up together really closely, and I could tell things from smells you wouldn't believe—like Mr. Phelps's dressing gown was more of a robe of office and the green box was in its pocket.

I meant to go over and sniff it, but I got waylaid by

the sofa. You know, if you dig your fingernails—I mean claws—into a sofa you can rush all over it, up and down and along the back, in seconds. Your tail whips from side to side and balances you. Then I jumped to the coffee table. It's so easy. You pick your place, just to the side of the cookie plate, and you sail halfway across the room, and you're there. I got ambitious then. I saw the mantel with a clock and ornaments on it, high up and right on the other side of the room. I aimed carefully. I waggled my back parts to get tuned up, and I sprang. I zoomed upward. And I did sort of get there with the front part of me. I had just an instant's glimpse in the mirror behind the clock of a fluffy black kitten with startled blue eyes, and then before I'd quite realized the kitten was me, I fell off. I turned over in the air and landed on my feet in the hearth, feeling cross.

"That will do, I think," said Miss Phelps's voice, high up, and zizzing and booming in my ears. "You must be used to yourself now."

Then I fell over sideways—*flip*!—and found myself on the mound outside the orphanage.

I understood almost at once why Mr. Phelps found it easier to time travel as a cat. The first thing I did was to stick up a black fluffy hind leg and wash it while I let my nose adjust me to everything around. I was sitting in rushes—no, grass—among forest trees covered with huge pale green, heart-shaped buds which I smelled out as the bushes on the mound. Lilac, probably. In the same instant, I knew it was a warm day in a different year, and that, though spring was much further advanced than the year I had come from, by the sun it was almost the same day of the year. The quarreling of the birds in the bushes made my mouth water. I stood up and thought about hunting.

An elegant grown-up black cat stood up, too, about a foot away. Mum makes a wonderful cat, like a small panther. As she stood up, a stripy tomcat came swaggering round the nearest forest bush and plainly decided that Mum was the next wife in his life. Tomcats are like that. "How about it, sweetheart?" he went in cat gestures.

Mum simply swung one velvet forepaw loaded with claws. *Scat!* A fast stabbing swipe that got the tabby hard over one ear. It was wonderful. Then she sauntered over to me, leaving the tabby cat crouched down with both ears flat. Poor Mr. Phelps. He was only behaving according to cat nature. So was Mum, I suppose. She gave me a swift rasping lick, to show the tabby she was still in charge of a kitten and not ready to be any cat's wife. Mr. Phelps backed to a respectful distance and then sat up, looking aloof.

Then we all realized that there were human voices coming from the field side of the mound. We'd been too occupied with cat business to notice before then. We all raced in that direction—using the low stealthy run, where you move each leg alternately like wading—until one of the little open paths gave us a view down into the field. Cats are perfect for hiding. Mum and I lay flat on our haunches. Mr. Phelps, like an old trouper, settled into a tuffet and doubled his front paws restfully under.

There were two humans down there. When we got there, they were doubled over in fits of laughter. One was a girl about Zenobia Bailey's age with long, long black hair, hanging loose and straight so that it hid what she was like. The other was a man who looked like a student to me—that sort of age, anyway.

"I don't think it's possible!" he said, as he stood up and tried to stop laughing. I nearly didn't recognize him, even then, not until he stopped laughing enough to be just smiling. Then I saw he had the same long, long grin as the ghost. He had light mouse-colored hair, and he did wear it longish and swept back, and his nose did have a slight bend to it, but it was not enough to make it like a parrot's beak. And his face only reminded you of a court jester if you had seen the ghost. I think Mum was right. The ghost was Antony Green's *idea* of himself, not what he really looked like. He looked almost normal, standing in the sun, in old-fashioned trousers, laughing with the girl.

"Can a person pass through death?" he said. "You mean, can a person pass through *earth,* don't you?"

The girl stood up and shoved her hair back. She had one of those long, gaunt faces fashion models used to have, and her clothes made me want to laugh, they were so out-of-date. I expect she was good-looking, but I didn't like her eyes. "You said it. Not me," she said. "I just talked of the tradition. I want to know if you really can increase your power by going into the earth. Don't you want to try?"

Antony Green shrugged. "Not really."

She laughed and patted his arm. "Well, I think you're perfect as you are. Let's forget all about it."

I got rather embarrassed to look then, because he grabbed her by her shoulders and said, "I'm not perfect. But I do love you, Naomi."

She kissed him and said, "Ah, but do you trust me? You go on a lot about men and women all being the same this way, but I don't think you trust me as I trust you, or you'd let me put you in that mound and call you out again."

"Then I'd better do it just to show you," said Antony Green. He smiled his long smile, the getting-out-of-things smile, and I didn't think he meant it.

But Mum did. She took off in a sort of tiger spring and went running down the mound. When she got to the grass of the meadow, she slowed down to a trot and sort of picked her way toward them.

"Oh, look, there's a cat," said Antony Green. He was

glad for the distraction.

Naomi glanced at Mum. "A black cat for luck," she said. Some of what I didn't like in her eyes was the way they calculated the use of things as they looked at them. Mum was useful. "To show you there's no harm in my test," she said.

Mum tried to show Antony Green that there *was* harm in it by weaving in figure eights round their legs. He looked down at her and said, "In America a black cat means the opposite. Bad luck."

"So you don't trust me," said Naomi. "After all your talk, you take the first excuse to back out."

"No, I don't," he said. "I'll do it. I told you." He bent and picked up a sort of green coat that had been lying in the grass till then. He sort of shrugged himself into it. It was long and full and dark green. He stood there grinning his long grin at Naomi. Suddenly he did look much more like the ghost. "On condition you do the same after me," he said.

There was that thing in Naomi's eyes again—a flash of calculation. "Yes, of course," she said. "The moment you come out."

She looked at him in a clear, truthful way then, and Antony Green tried to go on grinning, but it was the way you do when you have butterflies in the stomach. I saw he really was going to believe the beastly girl, and I dashed off down the mound to try and stop him.

"Oh, look!" he said. "There's a kitten now. What a beauty." He kneeled down and put his hand out for me to smell, to take his mind off what he was going to do. Smelling a human hand is a sort of an acquired taste for cats. I liked the way his smelled, but it made me sneeze. Mum came and barged against him warningly. "I'm not going to hurt your kitten," he said.

"No, just my feelings!" Naomi said. "You'd rather play with two cats than do a little simple thing for me."

Antony Green took back his hand and stood up. "It's not a simple thing," he said.

"Well, I know that, really," Naomi said hastily. "Trust isn't a little thing."

"That's why I'll do it," he said.

Mum and I sat side by side and stared at him. We both knew we had been no help at all. I sneezed again. The breeze had veered and there was a strong smell of Aunt Maria somewhere. The end of Mum's tail twitched, and I saw one of her ears turn to try for a sound to go with the scent.

"Are you going to do it or *not*?" Naomi said with real impatience.

"Starting now," said Antony Green. He took the green box from the pocket of his green coat, all shining and fascinating and bright. Mum's eyes followed it in amazement. He opened it just a fraction so that just one strong wisp of stuff escaped and swirled around him. "I wish you two wouldn't stare so," he remarked to Mum and me. "You put me off."

"A cat can look at a king," Naomi said, laughing.

"True," said Antony Green, and tried to give her the green box. She stepped back from it in a hurry. "Sorry," he said. "I forgot you don't like touching it." And he dropped it carelessly on the grass. Mum was so curious that she got up and sniffed at it. Neither of the humans noticed, because they were standing face to face.

Antony Green said, "By the power that is with me, I give you the right to call me from the earth, by my name and your name."

"And to put you in," Naomi prompted him.

"I'll do that for myself," he said. "I want to know if I can." Then he took the green coat off again—it was obviously a robe of office like Mr. Phelps's dressing gown—and dropped it on top of the box. "Here goes," he said. He made Naomi a nervous, friendly little face, the way I do to Chris on the diving board, and walked to the mound. "I *think*," he said, "like this."

I didn't see what "like this" meant, because Mum dashed off and I followed her, in a last futile effort to stop him. We ran more or less under his feet—he had suede shoes on—and we tripped him up. Or else he stumbled in order not to tread on us. The last sight I had of Antony Green was of him falling, rather like Miss Phelps did the first time, with one arm out in a sideways curve. There was no crashing of bushes or even the thump you might expect. He just fell through the budding branches and the grass and some of a muddy path and straight on into the side of the mound as if none of it was there. When I turned round in the bush we had fled through, there was no sign of Antony Green and no sign of any difference to the mound.

We crouched there watching Naomi walk to the place where he had vanished. She was smiling a little curve of a smile. She looked at the place carefully and nodded. Then she stretched both arms out and said equally carefully, "By the power vested in me, I hereby seal this mound and you into it. I lay it upon you to be there until I, Naomi Laker, call you out."

Then she practically ran back to the green coat to pick it up. "Ho, ho! Whoopee!" I heard her say.

Aunt Maria came running round the mound. She looked much the same, except she moved a good deal quicker, and she obviously shouted just as much then as she does these days. "You did it, dear! Oh, my dear child! Devoted artistic darling! I thought for a while you were never going to get him in. No one else in Cranbury could have induced him to!"

"The power of love, Mother," Naomi said.

"You're not *regretting* it, dear, are you?" Aunt Maria said, plunging forward to look in Naomi's face.

"Not in the least," Naomi said. "But it wasn't nice,

and it was hard work. I'm going to take the green box for my pains, at least."

"Why, dear?" said Aunt Maria. "You know you can't handle it."

"Neither can you," Naomi said. "Mother, dear, I think you should retire and let me take over. I've got twice your power now."

Aunt Maria started back with her hands to her chest and stared. Naomi smiled. The ribs of her face stood out. Her eyes were fanatical like Elaine's, blazing to find a weakness in Aunt Maria. Aunt Maria did her more-in-sorrow-than-anger voice. She's obviously practiced it for years. "I'm very hurt, dear. Very. I vested a great deal of power in you and named you to follow me. Isn't that *enough*?"

"Nope," said Naomi. "You're far too old-fashioned, Mother, and I want to start doing new things. And I noticed in your usual cunning way you pretended not to hear when I said I had the power. I have. The green box, for a start. That gives me the men. And I've got *him*." She pointed to the mound. "That means I've got you, too, because I've got the key to get him out. If you don't do what I say from now on, I shall simply open the mound. And he'll make you feel *very* bad, won't he, Mother, dear?"

"Viper," Aunt Maria said, using her failing-health voice. "Vicious girl. After all I've done for you!"

"Oh, shut up!" shouted Naomi. "Can't you stop pretending for an instant?"

Aunt Maria shouted, too. "Vicious, vulgar, loud-mouthed *monster*!"

They had a flaming row then, screaming at one another in the bright green field. Naomi screeched such things at Aunt Maria that I almost liked her. She yelled most of the things I've always wanted to say: "hypocritical hag" and "lazy old bag—I do *all* your chores for you!" But Aunt Maria yelled things about Naomi like "scarlet woman!" which were just as bad, probably. I bet they were true, too.

And right at last, Naomi screamed, "All right! *All* right! I'll say the word, and I'll fetch Green out this instant! *He'll* show you!"

Aunt Maria held up a quivering fist. "You *rotten* creature! Never another word, and not that word—ever! By the power vested in me, may you never use human speech again!"

And Naomi dropped down and seethed, just like Chris, and her old-fashioned clothes came off her, until she became a tall, gaunt wolf, snarling at Aunt Maria. She wasn't finished even then. She dropped low and came creeping as she snarled, ready to spring on her mother. Dribble was trailing from her open jaws.

"Back!" Aunt Maria said. "Back, you bitch! Go to Loup Woods, and may it mean your death if you ever set foot outside them."

So Aunt Maria brought it on herself, in a way. Mum and I both squashed ourselves to the ground, as the wolf Naomi raced across the mound, right past us, on the nearest way to the woods. I know how Lavinia felt when Chris was near now. It's rather like a human would feel if he or she went in the living room and found an escaped tiger in it.

Aunt Maria, meanwhile, didn't seem particularly sorry. Maybe she realized later. She picked up Antony Green's green coat and looked down at the box in the grass underneath. Then grunting, rather, she bent down and scooped the box up with the coat, into a bundle, so that she need not touch the box.

THIRTEEN

I felt huge and heavy and rather sad at being myself again. Mum was climbing into her jeans, Mum-shaped again.

"That poor, silly boy!" she was saying. "The stupid kid! Couldn't he see—?"

"Please get dressed, Margaret," Miss Phelps interrupted from her chair. "Nathaniel is waiting outside until you are decent. We have a lot to discuss."

I got dressed, and Mum continued to moan. "It was our fault, too, Mig. If we hadn't come down from the mound, he would have refused. I see *that* now."

"It would have happened, anyway," I said from inside my sweater. "It already had."

When Mr. Phelps came in, he was holding a clean white handkerchief to his face, and he backed me up. "There is never any way you can change the past," he said.

"I *was* hoping to do something," Mum confessed. "I thought—"

"But don't you see, ma'am?" said Mr. Phelps. He took the handkerchief away from his face and gestured with it. We all pretended that we couldn't see four long red claw marks down his left cheek. "Two cats came down the mound twenty years ago, which means that is what happened twenty years ago. You were always going to come down the mound because you already *had*."

"Please describe what happened," Miss Phelps said. "I wasn't there, you know."

So we told her. It took awhile. Mum interrupted to moan, or say things like, "They never considered poor Antony Green for a moment, did you notice, Mig? They never even seemed to think *he* was feeling anything." And Mr. Phelps annoyed us both by keeping saying, "I make it an absolute rule never to interfere with the past. That's much the safest way." During this, some people ran up the street. It was so unusual for Cranbury that I couldn't help noticing. One of them shouted, somewhere at the end of the street. Tut, tut, I thought. Then, with a nasty jolt, I thought, I do hope it wasn't Chris!

Mum said, "Well, I can't see what to do. Naomi put him in and she's dead now, I gather. And I do think he's suffered enough for his stupidity."

"Think a little," Miss Phelps directed us.

"Blessed if I can see—," Mr. Phelps said. The doorbell rang then. He said, "Curses!" and strode off to answer it. Miss Phelps tweaked the net curtain aside and looked out. It was obviously no one interesting.

She turned back to us and said, "I don't like to see hope abandoned. It seems to me that both of you had a hand—or should I say paw?—in putting the unfortunate young man where he is. Would that fit the terms?"

"No," said Mum, despairing. I wish she wasn't so emotional.

"Yes!" I said. "Mum, I'm called Naomi Laker, too."

Mum saw the point and jumped up. "Come on, Mig." She rushed to Miss Phelps and shook her little monkey hand. "Say good-bye to your brother for us. Thank you. We'll go to the mound now. We should be back in half an hour."

"It may not be so—," Miss Phelps said.

Mum had dragged me out into the hall by then. As she was opening the front door, someone said, "*Is* that so important then?" Mum turned and stared at me. "Of course it is!"

"I didn't say anything," I said. "It was one of the people Mr. Phelps let in just now."

"Oh, sorry," Mum said. She slammed the Phelpses' front door and we set off up the street.

Then we got lost—which is silly in a place as small as Cranbury—because I had never been to the orphanage by road and Mum had never been there at all. There is never anyone around to ask the way from. We found the sea twice, and we were coming up a small road from it the second time when we saw Zoe Green hurrying toward us, clutching her knitted blanket around her. Mad as she is, Mum rushed up to her in her eager social way and asked how we got to the orphanage.

There were tears pouring down Zoe Green's crushed turnip face. I found I was searching for something that was like Antony Green, but I couldn't see anything. But then I am not like Mum—though Chris is.

"Orphanage?" Zoe Green said. She waved blanket and arm the way we had come from. *"Carthago delenda est,"* she said. "Oh, my dearest Augustine, all is gone by."

She was even madder than usual. "Come on," I said to Mum, and we both hurried on. Mum made pop-eyed faces at me as we went. I don't think she had realized before how mad Zoe Green is.

The orphanage was just uphill from there. Before we got there, we could hear heavy engines and the sound of trees cracking. We looked at one another, wondering. When we turned the corner, we found the hedge missing from the side of the road and what looked to be most of the women in Cranbury standing with their backs to us gazing into the field where the mound was. We ran. We pushed in behind them.

"Extension for the orphanage, dear," said the lady from the clothes shop.

We looked over a flat space of mud and old tree roots, and saw two yellow excavators working on the mound. Half of it was gone already. The lilac bushes were lying this way and that on top, and their roots were sticking out of the reddish earth of the sliced side like twisted black wires. Everyone standing round leaned forward, staring intensely as the excavators moved in to cut another slice from it. I could see Aunt Maria in her wheelchair right in front of everyone, leaning forward as eagerly as anyone. One digger scooped another great chunk of mound away. The second chomped a slice from the exact place where Antony Green had fallen into the earth. We knew what everyone was looking for. We stared as eagerly as the rest, while that digger backed away, at the raw red piece of mound left. It was just earth and roots. Our eyes went to the load of earth the digger was carrying aloft then and watched urgently as it tipped with a slither and a crash on the earth piled at one side. But that seemed to be just earth, too.

"Nothing," the clothes shop lady murmured.

Mum backed into the road, pulling me. "I can't watch any more!" she said. "Let's go back to Miss Phelps. Quickly." We hurried down into the town again.

I said, "At least we didn't see a chopped arm or leg."

"But I think I saw a bit of cloth fluttering. I'm not sure," said Mum.

"Wouldn't this let him out?" I asked. But I knew from the way everyone had been eagerly looking that it was not like that.

"Nonsense," said Mum. "They were out to destroy him completely. Why not use spades if they weren't? Did you see Aunt Maria's *face*?"

We hammered at the door of number twelve and had to wait ages until Miss Phelps slowly, slowly opened it. "Ah, I thought you'd be back," she said.

"They're bulldozing the mound," I said.

"And we've got to act fast," Mum said, and whirled into the hallway. Miss Phelps fell over ushering me in, and Mum whirled back and caught her just in time. She kept hold of Miss Phelps and supported her back into the living room. I don't think Miss Phelps was pleased. She likes to do things for herself, including falling over. Mum is too used to Aunt Maria to realize. I shut the front door while Mum was saying, "Is your brother very busy? We need a very urgent council of war with both of you."

"Call him, Margaret," said Miss Phelps. "No, I can get into my chair unaided, thank you."

"Mr. Phelps!" I shouted.

Mr. Phelps was upstairs. He came stiffly hurrying down, looking as if he had just got out from under a shower. "What was the snag?" he said. And he hardly waited for me to answer before he stalked into the room. "I can't go this time," he said. "What time was it when you saw his projection last night? Don't stare, woman. Answer. It's important."

Mum said, "I didn't mean to seem stupid, but I don't understand."

Miss Phelps said, "My brother is somewhat ahead of himself. It is clear that if our friend is not to be destroyed by excavators, he will have to be removed some time between when you last saw him and the moment the workmen started to dig."

"Time travel, Mum," I said.

"Just a short way," said Miss Phelps. "My feeling is—just after dawn this morning. Do you all agree?"

This kind of thing is not Mum's strong suit. Her forehead wrinkled. "I . . . see," she said. "Then could we go as quickly as possible, please?"

"You could go this evening or tomorrow and still get there in time. Next year," said Mr. Phelps. "Women's brains alarm me. Totally obtuse. But if you would be happy going now, do so. I'm rather busy."

We had a last sight of him marching out of the room again as we went. I felt sick. Mum lurched against me, and we both shivered. Mum was still thinking of back in the future. She said, "Oh, dear, I'm afraid we interrupted him in something. I think his sister is *much* nicer. Good heavens! It really *is* dawn!"

It was. The sky was all pink. Mist hung across the field in bands, and the woods uphill were gray with it. The mound in front of us was black, wet, and dripping, except for the sparse white-green buds on the bushes.

"You want to wait a moment and adjust?" I asked. I did.

"When will the workmen be here? What time is it?" Mum said. She looked at her watch. Of course it said eleven-thirty. "Let's try now," she said.

We walked up to the mound. My feet got soaked in dew. It was getting lighter all the time, and I took a long look round, remembering this was the last time I'd see the mound and its bushes in the green field. I looked up at the woods, clearing out of the mist, and wondered where Chris was.

"Get on, Mig. You have to do it," Mum said, and looked at her watch again.

"I know," I said. "I'd better do it in the words she used, hadn't I?" Mum nodded. So I stretched out both hands and said, "By the power vested in me, I unseal this mound and . . . er . . . you from it, Antony Green."

"Say your *name,*" Mum hissed.

So I said, "This is Naomi Laker. I call you out, Antony Green."

There was a moment when Mum slumped, thinking it hadn't worked. Then we saw that the bushes were different nowadays. The right place was up and to the right a bit. The earth and bushes seemed to be milling into hundreds of transparent dots there. But they weren't moving, the dots. They were just going sort of unsolid to let a long pale figure rise out of them. He came to the surface just the way someone would come up from water, lying sideways, and lay for a moment along the mound, in the exact position he would have fallen in when we tripped him up. Then very slowly and shakily, he stood up.

"Oh, my God!" Mum whispered in dismay.

He was thin as a skeleton, and that made him seem about nine feet high. His hair had grown into a great mane. It was white now. So was the long scraggly beard on his chin. And in all those years, most of his clothes had rotted away, and the skin underneath was a horrible clayey white, too, and wrinkled and dirty. He stared at us and at the dawn breaking, and I noticed his eyebrows were still dark, in Vs upside down, like the ghost's.

"Who—who are you?" he asked in a voice that would hardly work. It sounded like wind blowing in a jug.

"We are Betty and Margaret Laker," Mum said.

That of course puzzled him dreadfully. He bent his face to think, and then of course he could see his beard and all the rest of his skeleton body. He looked up at us unbelievingly. "I'm old," said his creaky, windy voice. "What has happened?" He was horrified. He was too horrified to listen when Mum said, "Would you like to come with us?" He said, across her, "No! I'm old! What *happened*?"

And then he ran away. There was nothing we could do to stop him. He charged down the mound and ran like a stag across the field, in and out of the mist, waving his arms. It was like a scarecrow running. The tatters of his clothes streamed every time he waved his arms. They looked white when he disappeared into the first bank of mist. They seemed to be green when he came out.

"We'd better go after him," I said.

"Yes, in case he hurts himself. He's in shock, I think," Mum said.

We spent the rest of that morning trying to keep up with Antony Green. He was up in the woods about half the time, and we were climbing and slipping and panting, trying to keep sight of the crazy running, leaping scarecrow figure who always seemed to be going uphill from us. When I had breath, I shouted to Chris to come and help us with him. But no wolf appeared, and Antony Green bounded crazily on. Every so often he stopped, or we'd never have kept near him. Then he shouted things and the woods rang, bringing birds up in clouds. Or he did a mad leaping dance. Part of the dance seemed to be that his clothes changed color, though they were always in tatters. You never knew if you'd be chasing a green or a white or a red scarecrow next.

"Perhaps it's a ritual?" I panted. "Suppose we go down to the fields and wait until he comes down from the woods?"

Mum wouldn't hear of it. "He could break a leg any moment. Or he may not come out at all. I feel so responsible," she said.

"You *would*!" I snapped.

Antony Green came down from the woods of his own accord soon after that, and for a while he seemed even more crazy. He bounded across the field where the wolf had been shot and did his maddest dance yet in clear space among the cars in the station car park. This time his tatters turned several colors at once, like a jester's suit, and he waved long arms whirling white and black, red and green.

"He's as mad as his mother," I said as we limped down the field path.

"Is Zoe Green his mother? Oh, now I understand why she was so upset," Mum said, and she put on a limping spurt as if the thought of Zoe Green really inspired her. We just might have caught up with him there, if the booted porter hadn't come rushing out into the car park. We were too far away to tell if the porter was trying to stop Antony Green or what, but the madly whirling figure cavorted away from the porter's grabbing arms and went rushing off toward Cranbury Head.

Off we hobbled after him. We could see him leaping about on the road above the cliff while we were still at the edge of the houses.

"Mum," I said, "I know what he's doing. He's going all round Cranbury, sort of beating the bounds. Let him. We can stop him after that."

It did seem as if I was right, more or less. He came

down from Cranbury Head long before we got near it, and ran along the sand for a while, a bit more calmly, only skipping and waving every so often. Then he went off among the houses. Mum insisted that we keep him in sight, though, so we staggered on.

"Why is the town so empty? You'd think somebody would see him," Mum said.

I explained that, by this time, everyone would be at the excavation except the people who had gone to work. Mum looked at her watch. She couldn't cure herself of doing that. It now said nearly three o'clock, which puzzled her horribly.

"Now you have an idea how he must feel," I said.

We spotted him then, running much more slowly, away from us down the street where the drugstore is. We toiled behind him in a sort of dogtrot.

"He's slowing down, I think," Mum said. "We'd better take him to the Phelpses when we do catch him. He's really not responsible."

"Yes, but . . . ," I said. "I don't know if you're going to grasp this, Mum, but do try—at this precise moment *we* are at the Phelpses, you and I, discussing how to get him out. We can't go there. Because we didn't when we *were* there, do you see?"

"Yes, but we were away for hours being cats," Mum said. She looked at her watch again, as if that helped.

"No. We were probably only away for the time it took

to be sent and brought back," I said. "If your watch said eleven-thirty when we were at the mound at dawn—"

"Oh, don't!" said Mum. "It's worse than when we have to set the clocks forward!"

"All right. But if you look at your watch again, I shall scream," I said.

At that moment we came into Aunt Maria's street. Antony Green, ahead of us, began going faster. I groaned. He had a purposeful sort of look I dreaded now.

Mum said suddenly, "*Run,* Mig! He's on his way back to the mound. Stop him!"

I knew she was right. It was in the dream, somehow. He used to imagine himself out of his mound and dancing round Cranbury, just like he had been doing, but he always came to himself to find he was in the mound. So he thought that was where he should be now. And that meant he would walk straight into Aunt Maria's arms.

By then I didn't think I could run another step, but I did. Mum and I pelted down the street. Antony Green heard us. He glanced back and began to run faster, too. I thought I was going to burst. Mum almost did. At the end of the street she gave up and leaned on a house. Antony Green was just turning up the street that led to the orphanage.

"Stop!" I yelled. And Mum screamed at him, "Antony Green! Stop. Come here, you fool!"

He stood still, facing away from us.

"Come back here, and I'll explain!" I called.

He turned round and came toward us, very hesitatingly, clutching his rags around him. He was limping, too. He had changed himself a little while he had been running. He still looked like a mad Robinson Crusoe, but he didn't look so old as he had. His beard was shorter and streaked with darker hair, though his mane was still white.

"What is it you want of me?" he said. He was panting, but his voice was like a real person's now.

"Just to see you safe," Mum panted. "What do you say to going to see Nathaniel Phelps?"

"I could do," he said, rather surprised. "He lives in this street, doesn't he? Is he still alive? How long have I been underground?"

"You've only lost twenty years," Mum said. "Though I daresay it seemed like centuries to you."

We both stared at Antony Green anxiously, wondering how insane this would make him. "*Only!*" he said. "That's one way of looking at . . . " Then he looked at us, really looked at us for the first time. "I know you both," he said. "From a dream I had a short while back."

"That's right," I said. "*Please* come to the Phelpses. I've lost track of what the time really is, and I don't want Aunt Maria to find you."

He came with us quite obligingly then, and we rang

at the door of number twelve. Mr. Phelps opened it. He stared. He glanced over his shoulder to the door of the living room. "In," he said. "All of you. In at once." We crowded into the hall, and the huge skeletal shape of Antony Green towered over Mr. Phelps as well as us. Mum moved forward to open the living-room door, but Mr. Phelps opened the door on the other side of the hall. "In, in, in," he said, and fairly bundled us through it. "Not in there," he whispered. "You are already in there at the moment, your former selves. You mustn't meet."

At that moment we heard the door of the living room burst open and hasty feet in the hall. It gave me a queer feeling.

"*Is* that so important then?" Mum said. So that was who said it.

The front door slammed. "It may be," Mr. Phelps said. "I didn't want to take the risk." Then he looked at Antony Green, who was standing, hanging his head, and asked, "Is he . . . all right?"

He didn't look all right, but Mum said, "Yes, of course. He wants food and a bath and clothes and—listen, if Mig and I just went out the front door, won't there be two of each of us ever after?" Mr. Phelps looked at the ceiling and clenched his jaw.

"Oh, God, Mum!" I said. "And don't forget to look at your watch, too."

Antony Green laughed. "No," he said. "Your earlier

selves will just move round to the point where you went into the past. They are *you*, after all."

It sounded utterly sane. It looked as if Mum had accidentally said the right thing. She went on being accidentally helpful, too, because she really was puzzled. Mr. Phelps fetched food to the dining room we turned out to be in. All the time I was eating my share as hungrily as Chris, Mum was asking about time travel and Antony Green was telling her, quite clearly and sanely. But he couldn't eat much.

"My stomach's shrunk," he said. "It was bound to, I suppose."

Miss Phelps came shuffling in and shook hands shyly with him. "I'm pleased to see you back," she said. "But I can't stay long. Margaret and her mother will be back shortly."

"But we're here!" said Mum. She was hopeless.

After that Mr. Phelps took Antony Green upstairs to have a bath. The bathroom was over the dining room. We could hear tremendous splashing, mixed with a lot of loud, unhappy laughter and Mr. Phelps barking orders that weren't listened to.

"He's gone dotty again," I said.

The doorbell rang. We heard Miss Phelps shuffling to answer it. Now I knew why Miss Phelps said, "Ah, I thought you'd be back." I didn't know I sounded so wimpish. Then our earlier footsteps went into the living room. Shortly mine came racing out again, and my wimpish voice yowled, "Mr. Ph—elps!" All this while there were such splashings and yellings from the bathroom that I couldn't understand how we hadn't heard them the first time we were there.

As soon as Mr. Phelps came downstairs, Mum dived for the door. "I don't think he should be left alone," she said. She raced upstairs and I raced after her, whispering, "Mum! Mum, it's not our house!" and trying to make her stop.

Actually, Antony Green was quite all right. He was sitting up to his neck in bubble bath with his beard trailing in the foam, building the bubbles into shapes. When we came in, he gave us his long grin, put out a skinny arm, and touched the nearest pile of bubbles. All the piles of foam took on faint, misty color. You could suddenly see they were hills and fields, with castles on the hills and clusters of little houses in the dips. It was like when you see landscapes in your bedclothes.

Mum said, "Good heavens! That's beautiful."

I said, "You ought to come out now. You've gone all wrinkly."

Then Mr. Phelps came back, and he was terribly shocked to find us in the bathroom. He made us go out onto the landing and shut the bathroom door. Then he began barking orders again.

"I wish he'd stop. That's not the way to manage

him," Mum said, leaning her ear to the door. "I wish he'd let me."

"I don't think people should manage people at *all,*" I said.

"Yes, but he's treating him like a *child*!" Mum said, not listening.

I leaned gloomily on the banister, wondering how I would ever get Chris turned back to a boy now that Antony Green was mad, until Mr. Phelps threw open the bathroom door and said, "Do either of you cut hair? He won't let me touch it."

"We could try," Mum said.

Antony Green was sitting on a cork-topped stool looking halfway normal. His body was in neat fawn trousers and sweater, but his head looked like a shipwrecked pirate's. He was staring at himself in the bathroom mirror. "Raggedy Andy," he said.

"Robinson Crusoe," I said.

"Do you want to stay like that?" Mum said.

He gave us a long, wondering grin. "I *am* like that," he said. "Can I change?"

"You changed yourself while you were dancing round Cranbury," I said.

"Hush, child," said Mr. Phelps. He kept trying to stop me talking about things like that. He said, "Hush!" every time I mentioned the mound or any of the mad things Antony Green had done, but Antony

Green didn't mind, and Mum didn't try to stop me.

"I could cut the beard off," he said, looking in the mirror.

"I wish you would," I said. "It looks awful."

"And my hair?" he asked.

"Yes," said Mum and I.

"Then could you find some scissors, Nat?" Antony Green asked. Mr. Phelps looked at the ceiling and took a pair of scissors out of his dressing-gown pocket. He held them toward Mum, but Mum waved to him to give them to Antony Green. Mr. Phelps raised his eyebrows, but he put the scissors into Antony Green's pale, withered hand. Antony Green looked at the scissors uncertainly for a moment, then he said, "I'd be grateful for a bit of help, really."

So Mum cut his hair and his beard. He looked quite a bit better like that. I think his hair was sort of bleached by the earth, because it was much darker near the roots. Or maybe he turned it darker. When it was done, he looked at himself again and said he ought to shave the beard right off. So we all pothered around for Mr. Phelps's shaving things. In the midst of the pother, I began to suspect we had simply swapped looking after Aunt Maria for looking after Antony Green.

"Don't be unfair, Mig!" Mum said. "It's not a bit the same. You can't expect someone who's been buried alive to get over it in half a day!"

"I don't suppose he ever will," I said. "And how are we *ever* going to get Chris back now?"

We were unwisely whispering this in the bathroom doorway. While I was saying that, we both realized that Antony Green must have heard. He was staring at us with the razor poised and half his face covered with white cream. We stared back guiltily.

"The two black cats!" Antony Green said. "I knew I'd seen you somewhere else before that dream! You were trying to warn me, weren't you?"

I said, "Yes. And we sent you into the mound by tripping you up." Mr. Phelps was bustling jerkily about, picking up every bit of Antony Green's hair in a ritualistic kind of way, and he of course began shushing me. But I took no notice and said, "Would you have stayed out and realized about Naomi, if we hadn't done that?"

"No, I don't think so," Antony Green said. "There's no need to feel guilty about it." He turned back to the mirror and began shaving himself again. He said the rest in jerks, while he was dipping the razor in water or twisting his face sideways to see if he had got all the beard off the sides. "I was besottedly set on it, I'm afraid. It wasn't only Naomi's doing. I wanted to force her to be trustworthy—I didn't realize that if people really can trust one another, it doesn't need proving. I only saw that"—he paused, scraping the place under his funny bent nose, to say this—"some rather long months later."

"But you did love Naomi," I said. "And I'm afraid she's—"

"Hush!" said Mr. Phelps.

"Dead," said Antony Green quite calmly, turning his face up to do under his chin. "I know she must be, or I wouldn't be out. I saw what she was like quite early on . . . when an hour had passed and I was still underground. But her mother's still alive, isn't she?"

"Yes!" Mr. Phelps said, in an angry explosion.

"But something else happened," said Antony Green. He seemed to turn saner and saner as he talked. Maybe it was the sight of his own face coming out of the lather. It wasn't a usual face, and it was awfully thin, but wasn't the mad castaway's face, or the court jester's face of the ghost, either. It was sort of halfway between those and the face of the young man who had bent down and held out his hand to me as a kitten. "Something gave me an access of strength a short while back," he said. "I was almost done for by then. But I suddenly began to be able to project and dream and time travel again."

Mr. Phelps gave me a meaning glare. "Oh," I said. "Me. I opened the green box and a lot of the stuff got out."

Antony Green caught my eye in the mirror. "Thank you," he said. "Your brother's a wolf, isn't he?"

See what I mean about him getting saner? "How do you know?" I said.

"I saw you with him in that room," he said. "I'd gone back to the present by then. First of all, I homed in on the green box and tried to find it. It was in that room for years, and I went doggedly through the years, trying to find someone there with it who might help me. I'd worked back to about four months ago, before there was anyone in the room at all, and then unfortunately there was Gregory Laker—"

"Dad," I said. "What did he do?"

"Took the box away," Antony Green said. "I managed to make him understand—I thought. But perhaps he didn't. He got very excited."

If Antony Green could accept hard facts, I thought I could. "He wanted it himself," I said. "He envied you. He told me." Mum sat on the edge of the bath and looked unhappy. I said, mostly to make her feel better, "Aunt Maria got at him after that, and I think he forgot he'd seen you."

"So I had to try again," Antony Green said. He finished shaving and turned round to talk after that. "Something *had* happened, because I still thought the green box was in that room. I found the next person by daylight—an elderly woman I didn't know—who was making up the bed."

"Lavinia?" Mum asked me.

"I scared her silly," Antony Green said. "She began laughing hysterically and ran out of the room shouting,

'Mrs. Laker! You did some poor fellow in, didn't you? I'm not staying with you one moment longer!' And I never saw her again."

"She's a cat now," I said.

"So then I found your brother," said Antony Green. "I'd just begun to make him understand, and I was almost at my last gasp, when I realized he was a wolf, and you were there." The way he said this made me see that the nights must have run together for Antony Green. I suppose they would if you were lying underground. He frowned a bit and said, "I must put that right at once."

"Oh, bless your heart!" Mum said.

fouRteeN

They went to find Chris, but I stayed behind. I was sitting on the edge of the Phelpses' bath nine-tenths asleep by then. Mum didn't seem to notice that two mornings in succession add up to a whole day. There is that advantage to not understanding time travel. She was fresh as a daisy. And I hadn't done credit to how worried she was about Chris. She said to Antony Green, "I could have screamed all the time you were careering round the town! I kept thinking of poor Chris."

He gave her his long, mischievous, getting-away-with-it grin. "I am sorry."

"No, you're not," said Mum. "You were enjoying yourself. Not that I blame you."

Antony Green was fresh, too, in a calm, easy way. I supposed as I nodded on the edge of the bath that he had had twenty years to rest in, but now I think it was more than that. He had something within him, now that he was sane. He turned to Mr. Phelps and held out a hand. "I'll take the green box, Nat."

Mr. Phelps took the wonderful flashing, glowing box out of his pocket and plonked it into Antony Green's hand, very hastily, as if it hurt him to touch it. Then he bustled to the bathroom cupboard and came back with the big green highwayman's-coat kind of robe. It smelled of mothballs. "I rescued this from the woods," he said.

Antony Green looked up from running his fingers gently over the patterns on the box, and his long grin was rather bemused. It often is, actually. "Thanks," he said. "But I don't think I'm quite ready to reassume that yet. Can you keep it here and make people think I'm here with it?"

He opened and shut the box a tiny bit as he said it. Mr. Phelps gave a pained gasp at the waste and said, "Certainly. But—"

"I'm going to disappoint you, Nat, I know," Antony Green said. "I always did, rather, didn't I? I had time to think underground. And I'm not sure I care for our way of doing things here. Men's ways with the power shut in the box. Women's ways with the virtue hoarded in the Queen—"

"*Virtue!*" Mum said. She almost exploded at the idea. "How can you *sit* there—! After all you've been through, how *can* you sit there and call Auntie virtuous?"

"It means something different, Mum," I said.

Antony Green turned to Mum, sort of kindly. "Yes, it does," he said. "It's an old use of the word, meaning a certain kind of power. It's been our word for it in Cranbury for centuries. It goes back to the time when somebody here decided that men and women were different sorts of people and the rules for the ways they used the power should be different. That was early in the Middle Ages, I think. They divided into men's ways and women's ways then, and they've been making up more and more rules ever since to make the difference seem even bigger. Women allowed men the strong, out-of-doors things—provided the men put the virtue of their thoughts and ambitions into the box so that it couldn't get loose and run wild—while the men gave over all the secret, indoors things to the women—on condition the main power was kept safe by just a few strong women who would work by the rules. Those are the ones we call the Queens."

"You make it all sound like an anthill," Mum said.

"It is," he said, "particularly when it goes as wrong as it seems to have done these last twenty years. And the whole arrangement is nonsense, anyway. I want everyone to be free to use the power as they need to. The stuff in this box was once the birthright of every living soul in the world, you know."

Mr. Phelps stood to attention in a loyal way and said, "It's my place to follow you, Antony. I understand."

"You don't, Nat," Antony Green said.

It was about this point that I went to sleep and fell into the bath. Mum realized how tired I was and I got bundled along to Miss Phelps's bed. "We'll be back soon with Chris," Mum said. "You have a rest, Miggie. You've done valiantly."

I went to sleep for a bit, I don't know for how long. It was still broad daylight when I woke up, and I think it was early afternoon. The house was quiet except for some gobbling snores from somewhere. I woke up realizing that we weren't going back to Aunt Maria's and that all my things were in her house. What will Mum do without her pea green knitting? I thought. And there's my *writing*! I knew it would be a real disaster if Aunt Maria found my locked book and read all I had written about her. I knew I just had to get it back.

I was so worried that I got up and ran downstairs. I went into the living room to tell Miss Phelps about my writing. But she was curled up on the sofa like a rather big, gnomish baby, fast asleep. It was quite reasonable that she should be asleep. She'd had a busy morning. It never occurred to me to wonder. I tiptoed out and let myself softly out through the front door.

I told myself I would just sneak in through the back door. Aunt Maria was deaf, after all. If I was quiet, I could go in and out without her hearing a thing.

Well, I sneaked in. There wasn't a sound as I opened the kitchen door. I crept through the empty dining room across empty squares of sun lying on the dismal carpet. It never occurred to me that this was odd. At that time of day, the room ought to have been full of Mrs. Urs, clustered round the silver teapot. But I didn't think of that. I tiptoed through the hall and raced quietly upstairs, feeling very pleased with myself. My locked book, instead of being hidden under the bedroom carpet, was lying out on the bedroom table. Somehow that didn't worry me at all. I got Mum's pea green knitting out and put it carefully on the bed to remind me to take it, too. Then I sat down and unlocked my book. There is such a lot I have to put down now! I thought.

I sat there, and I wrote and wrote. It was very odd. I remembered exactly what had happened and what it meant to me at the time, and I knew it was real and urgent, but I never seemed to notice it was stupid to sit and write about it in Aunt Maria's house. I put down all about the wolf hunt, and I remember I got very impatient at how long that took, because I had all about Antony Green to put down, too, but it never occurred to me to connect it with the way I was behaving now.

Then when the light was getting a bit dim, I looked up with a jump to see a tall black figure standing in the doorway. It was Elaine. "Come downstairs," she said. "Your aunt wants to speak to you."

My heart kind of squeezed. I could hardly breathe

for sheer terror. When I stood up, my knees would hardly hold me.

Elaine walked to the table and picked up my open book. "I'll have that," she said. I remember my pen softly thudding on the carpet as she said, "If you are going to pour your thoughts out on paper, you ought to hide your scribbles in a better place. I found this in two seconds flat. You are a rude little beast, aren't you? I hope she makes you pay for some of the things you said." Then she marched me out of the room and down the stairs, holding me in her policeman's grip. As we were going down, she asked, "Where's your mother?"

Terror was roaring in my ears, but I had just sense to say, "No idea. She went off without me."

"I'll go and round her up later," said Elaine. She shoved me into the living room and shut the door after me.

"Come and sit down, dear," Aunt Maria said. She was sitting on her roped-up state sofa with a low pink lamp cozily lighting up her face. Her sticks were lying propped beside her, as if she didn't intend to use them. But they were there in case of emergencies. She pointed to the little armchair drawn up facing the sofa. "Dear little Naomi," she said. "I love talking to you, dear." She had her most kindly teddy-bearish look. It really was hard to see her without thinking of her as cuddly and lovable.

Elaine was clanking about in the hall somewhere as I

sat down. There was no chance of getting away. I stared at Aunt Maria's sweet, rosy face, and I had a sudden understanding of how Zoe Green had gone mad. Here were all these peculiar and awful things going on, and you knew all about them and wanted to scream and yell and cry, and yet here was Aunt Maria, so gentle and cuddly and civilized that you couldn't quite believe the awful things were happening. You felt guilty just thinking about them. You felt guiltier believing the awful things were true. As Aunt Maria began talking, I really began thinking something must be wrong with *me* for imagining she was wicked in the least.

She talked and talked. Mad and improbable though it seems, most of what she said was exactly the same as the usual things: what Adele Taylor had said to Hester Bailey—who paints such *gifted* pictures, dear—and what both of them had said to Benita Wallins. And on and on, about all the other Mrs. Urs. I remember having a little fleeting underneath thought that the main spell Aunt Maria cast was boredom. I kept having little fleeting thoughts. They were like little jabs of sanity in a vast, numb desert of boredom, as Aunt Maria's voice went on and on. You have to listen to her. She has this way of saying, "Listen, dear. This is really *interesting*!" And you do, and it's always the most boring thing yet.

Elaine began vacuuming the hall at some point, making another droning in my ears. One of my little jabbing thoughts was, She's a fool to leave Larry alone now Antony Green is out. But it didn't make any difference to the way I sat having to listen. My ears and my mind got blurred, so that I almost didn't catch the important things as Aunt Maria said them. They were sort of slipped in among the droning.

"Dear, you have really hurt me, but we shan't talk of that. I love my little new Naomi, and I know she loves me. . . . " Then she went on in a sighing way about how beautiful and gentle the old Naomi was, and what a brilliant mind she had. "*You* have a brilliant mind, too, dear," she said. And I had a jabbing thought that it was no wonder Naomi tried to get the better of Aunt Maria. She must have been sick of her.

Then after desert miles of more talk, I realized Aunt Maria was saying, "It hurt me to find you didn't trust me, dear. Hurt me very much indeed that you went and looked for your father by yourself. I was saving him as a wonderful surprise for you, for when you understood. I'm sure you understand now that he had to pass through death so that he could use the funny little box properly. I hope you and he and I will be working closely together in future. . . . "

So that's it! I thought. But Antony Green has been through death, too.

But I still didn't understand that Aunt Maria meant me to be her successor, not until ages more droning on about Mrs. Urs, when Elaine's vacuum cleaner went through into the dining room. Aunt Maria lowered her voice and leaned forward. "So Ann Haversham went to Selma Tidmarsh and they agreed to look after Elaine for me. Poor Elaine is very jealous, you know. She wanted to step into my Naomi's place. But I had already chosen you, dear, years ago, as soon as your father first brought you here to see me. It's a pity your father and mother don't get on. I brought you all here to reunite you. And of course I sent Lavinia away so that you could be one of the thirteen just as soon as you were ready."

I sort of fizzed with horror as soon as she said that. Be one of the Mrs. Urs! Be like Elaine! I felt sick. I truly didn't hear the next bit of droning. When I next attended, Aunt Maria was chuckling at me in a roguish, matey way.

"So this is really your first lesson, dear. Do you understand how it's done? The main spell is just talk, and that's quite easy, but of course you are working away underneath the talk, putting all sorts of things into people's minds and tying their thoughts into the right shape. This is something you'll learn in time. It takes time. I wish you could have been there when I had my long talk with poor Zoe Green. That was me at my best."

I stared at her. I couldn't believe it.

"Ah, yes, dear. You do understand," Aunt Maria said. "The power is vested in you. It tore loose from poor

Naomi when the men made that mistake over her. I felt you take it on yourself early this morning. You do understand, dear."

Oh, no! I thought. In order to let Antony Green out, I had to be one of *them*! Why didn't I realize?

"I think you're tired now, dear," Aunt Maria said. And I was. I went to sleep on the spot. I don't know what happened after that, except that I woke up next morning in the orphanage.

It was a little gray room with one little gray window looking out onto the foggy woods. What woke me was the sound of the excavators starting up to finish leveling the mound. That told me at once where I was. Even if I hadn't heard them, the smell would have told me—like a school really, only thicker and chillier. I jumped up. The first thing I saw was my old mildewy exercise book lying on the gray locker by the bed and a pen beside it. "The Story of the Twin Princesses." I grabbed it up and opened it, and found Aunt Maria's note written under the title on the first page. She has teddy-bearish writing. I knew the note was meant to make me feel humble and contrite. But it didn't. There were no spells on me now. I suppose if I was going to be her new Naomi, I had to have my own free will. I went and tried the door.

It wasn't locked. I stormed out into the gray corridor and came face to face with Phyllis Forbes. Her pink schoolgirl face was rather irritable.

"Didn't you hear the bell?" she said. "Get up at once, you lazy girl. Breakfast is half finished."

"Why should I?" I said. "I don't belong here."

"You do now," she said. "Get dressed or starve."

I was hungry. My clothes were on a chair. I went back in the room and dressed and Phyllis Forbes stood over me. I hated her. But I hated her much more by the end of breakfast.

The orphans were all downstairs in a long gray room quietly eating Muesli and drinking watery milk from plastic glasses. Phyllis Forbes shoved me down at a bench by the nearest long table and went stamping off. The orphans all looked at me with identical solemn clone expressions. They were all younger than me. That made me rather dejected.

"Don't just sit there. *Do* something!" I called out at them. "You all got filled with stuff from the green box. It must have made *some* difference!"

They just stared, and their eyes all shifted in unison to Zenobia Bailey. She was dressed like a nurse, in the same way as Phyllis Forbes. She hustled up, clacking her shoes, and clapped a bowl of Muesli down in front of me. "Milk's in the jug," she said. "Spoons in the box there."

"Do you work here?" I said.

"I give my time three mornings a week," she said. She sounded very righteous.

I wondered if she recognized me. "How generous," I

said. “Do you give people anything but Muesli? I hate Muesli. It's like mouse doo.”

“You'll eat it,” she said. “It's nourishing.”

“No, I won't. I'll throw up,” I said. “How about a crust of dry bread, instead?”

Zenobia Bailey sighed. “Phyllis!” she called out in a weary voice. “There's one being ornery here.”

Phyllis Forbes came zooming along the gray room and glared at me. “Oh, yes,” she said. “This one will be. She has much too good an opinion of herself. Are you going to eat up like a good girl?” she said to me.

“No,” I said. “I hate Muesli.”

“Then you'll eat it all up,” she said with a little sort of smile.

And I somehow had to. I spooned the spiky gray mush up, and choked, and spooned again, and the raisins seemed even more like dead flies than usual, but I still had to eat them. Phyllis Forbes hadn't done anything to my feelings. She had just put a sort of transparent bag around them, so that they bulged and struggled inside where I couldn't get at them. I had to sit dutifully there eating Muesli.

When I'd finished, she clapped her hands. “Come along now, children,” she called. “Activity time.” All the orphans got up obediently and filed out of the gray room, while she stood against the wall with her arms folded, watching. Elaine isn't Aunt Maria's only policewoman, I thought. I got up and went over to her.

"What is activity time?" I said. Then I burped Muesli and thought I was going to be sick.

She gave me a malicious smile. "The boys go for gymnastics," she said. "The girls have dancing. It trains the muscles."

"I want to do gymnastics," I said.

"But you'll do dancing," she said. "That's what young ladies do. This way."

I knew she could make me, so I went where she pushed me, looking as rebellious as I dared.

"In there. Take that look off your face. It won't do any good," she said.

It was a bare room with girl orphans standing around in it. The Mrs. Ur called Ann Haversham was sitting at a piano in one corner. "Is everyone here?" she called out.

I went over to her. "Do you give your time three times a week, too?" I said.

"Every day, dear," she said. "Stand with the others."

"Then you should ask to be paid," I said. "This is a slave farm."

She took no notice and called out, "Now, I want you all to be fairies!" She played little skittish fairy notes on the piano. I went and stood against the wall to watch the girl orphans running with little steps and fluttering their arms. Then I realized that Phyllis Forbes was standing against the wall, too, on the other side of the room.

Phyllis Forbes gave me another of her nasty smiles.

I found I had to dance, too. The plastic bag was over my feelings again. I felt huge and silly as I ran and flittered and then skipped in time to the fairy music. I was enormous compared with the other girls. I got angrier and angrier, but the plastic bag held my feelings in, and all I could do was bulge about inside. I knew how Chris had felt when he said awful things to Aunt Maria. As we all started waving our arms with sickening grace, the Muesli felt like a big gray clod in my stomach, and I felt worse still. Yet Antony Green danced, I thought. That was to express his feelings. Then I thought, I was filled with stuff from the green box—more than any of the orphans were—*and* I took on the power Aunt Maria had vested in Naomi, even if I didn't know I had. So I must be strong enough to do something. I made a great effort. And the plastic bag split, and I began to dance like Antony Green, leaping and whirling, kicking up my legs, and holding my arms high. It was a lovely feeling. The orphans stopped dancing and stared at me.

The music stopped. Phyllis Forbes came diving across the room and snatched hold of my arm. It hurt. "You wicked, graceless, indecent girl!" she said. "Now you shall be punished!"

I tried to look at her in a way that showed I was as strong as she was. But she was hurting my arm and I couldn't. So I said, "It's not punishment, whatever you do, because you enjoy watching people's feelings bulge, don't you?"

She dragged me out of the room, hurting my arm even more. "I shall break your spirit!" she said.

"You'd enjoy that, wouldn't you?" I gasped. But when someone is stronger than you in their muscles it is very hard to do anything. She dragged me all the way upstairs and threw me back into the gray room.

"You'll stay there without food until you're ready to behave!" she said. And she slammed the door and locked it. I suppose it was lucky she made me eat the Muesli.

Actually, I didn't write very much between the lines of "The Twin Princesses." I didn't dare. I wrote the first bit so as to defy everyone, and then my arm hurt too much where Phyllis Forbes had wrenched it. I sat on the bed, staring at the woods through the window, rubbing my arm and holding my eyes very wide to make the tears in them go away. I began to think my spirit probably *was* broken.

Then there was a soft little grating noise at the door of the room. My eyes went that way. I saw a cracker coming through the crack under the door. A second cracker was being pushed under a bit further along. It was the orphans. I thought I would stay sitting on the bed, but I didn't. I went over to the door.

"Thank you," I said. "Why are you doing that?"

"We always do that when one of us is being punished," one of them whispered from the other side of the door. "Bye for now." Feet softly scuffled away.

I still felt far too full of Muesli and rage to eat, but I picked up the crackers and hid them in the mattress in order not to get the orphans punished, too. More crackers kept arriving all morning. The bed crunched when I sat on it. I was just dismally thinking I had better sit on the floor and eat the crackers later on for supper, when I saw something moving in the wood out of the window. I looked, and whoever it was slid out of sight behind some bushes.

Funny, I thought. That looked like Larry Mr. Elaine.

I went to the window, and I was in time to catch sight of one of the boatmen scampering sideways to another bush. Not Chris again! I thought. Then I looked up at the woods and saw people coming down among the trees, three of them. One was Mum, sturdily marching with her hands in the pockets of her anorak. It was cold and still a bit foggy out there. Antony Green was with her, and he was wearing his green highwayman coat. The third person was Chris. He was a boy again and his clothes must have come from Larry, because they were just a bit big all over. They all came down the field until they vanished behind the high wall of the orphanage, but Mum had started to run by then.

I waited and I listened, and I never knew quite what

happened. I heard a huge bang, as if a heavy door had been slammed open and hit the wall beside it hard. The floor trembled a bit. Then I heard Mum. I couldn't hear what she was saying, but I could hear her. When Mum really gets going, it's quite hard to hear anything else. And she was really going. I stood in the middle of the room and listened to doors slamming, things going flying, other voices trying to interrupt Mum, and Mum's voice coming closer and closer and louder and louder. There was shouting, too, from the orphans. I could somehow hear they were cheering Mum on. Then there were a host of footsteps and Mum's voice, nearer and nearer, "I tell you she's my daughter and you have no *business* to shut her up here!"

Then the key scraped and my door crashed open, and there was Mum in a crowd of excited orphans, hauling Phyllis Forbes by the collar of her nurse's uniform.

"She's not harmed—," Phyllis Forbes started to say.

"Not harmed!" said Mum. "Just *look* at her!" I was so glad to see Mum that I had somehow started crying without knowing I had. Chris says he did, too, when Antony Green turned him back to a boy. "Not *harmed*!" Mum bellowed. "Why, you wicked, cruel woman!" And to my utter joy she banged Phyllis Forbes's head on the doorjamb. From the look of Phyllis Forbes, Mum had done that several times before, but when I asked Mum she said, "I don't know what I did, cherub. It was all a red mist. I was only thinking of getting you out of there."

I rushed up to Mum. Mum slung Phyllis Forbes aside and hugged me. The orphans shouted, "Lock Mrs. Forbes up now!"

Mum was obviously tempted, but she said, "No, we're getting out of here. Come on, all of you. Thank you for showing me where Mig was."

We left Phyllis Forbes sitting in the corridor and hurried downstairs in a crowd of yelling orphans to the front hall. The big front door was off its hinges, making a sort of frame for a knot of men, Larry among them, and Chris standing with Antony Green. I wondered why they hadn't come in. But both of them, for different reasons, were finding it hard to go indoors just then. When Chris saw me, he did actually come about three steps into the hall. I didn't realize then what a sacrifice that was. He dragged me back outside, both of us saying excitedly, "Tell me, tell me, tell me!"

There Antony Green smiled his long, sly, friendly smile at me. Beyond Larry and the men was another knot of men, the ones who had been working the excavators. Someone told me later they came from Minehurst way and didn't have a clue. But they knew something was going on. They stared like anything at me, all tear stained, and again at Mum. Mum came sailing out, surrounded by orphans. "You did mean to bring these, too?" she called.

"Oh, yes," said Antony Green. "Let's go." And he led

the way out through orphanage grounds and everyone else followed, like the Pied Piper's procession. Antony Green looks a bit like I always imagine the Pied Piper, anyway, and he was more like him than ever with Chris and me and all the orphans crowding after him.

"Where did Larry and the others come from?" I whispered to Chris.

"They were waiting in the woods when we came down this morning," Chris said. "They had clothes for me and that green coat for him, and they seemed to know all about everything. Larry went up to Antony Green and—do you know!—he bowed. 'You may not remember me,' he said. 'I was only ten when you were put down, but I've tried to keep things going the way you would have wanted.' Then he handed over the green coat."

"He wants to be the next Mr. Phelps," I said. "I bet. Tell me how they found you."

Chris wasn't sure. He thought maybe he found them. He said he was miles inland, as far as he could get, because roaming by night was one of the things he got to like about being a wolf. But he could never get enough of it. He always got more and more scared and uncertain the farther he ran from Cranbury. I think there was an injunction on him. Anyway, near dawn, he suddenly got a feeling that he had to go to Loup Woods at once. So he set off trotting. Quite a lot of people saw him. A man in a tractor tried to run him down in a field, and Chris was very scared and tired at being out by daylight. He was glad when he ran into sea mist and found the barn where he had taken to sheltering at the edge of Loup Woods. He crawled in through a gap in the back, and there was Mum, lying asleep on the straw where Chris usually slept.

"I couldn't believe it. I nosed at her," Chris said.

Mum was walking with an arm round both of us. She laughed. "I yelled," she said. "Poor Chris! He jumped back looking so scared. And I said, 'Chris! It's all right. I do know you. It's just your *nose* is so cold!' Then Antony came in."

"He said, 'Hello, Chris. I'm sorry this has happened to you,' and turned me straight back," Chris said.

"What? Just like that?" I said.

"Well, no mumbo jumbo or anything," Mum said. "He put a hand on Chris's head. Things were shadowy for a moment, and then he was standing with his hand on Chris's *real* head, and Chris was shivering all over. Poor Antony. He was sweating by then. He can't bear even being under a roof. And Chris is as bad."

"Now you tell us about the orphanage," Chris said.

"But you haven't told me about the hunt," I said. Our procession was going along the promenade by then, with the sea swelling all soft and gray and foggy to one side.

"That'll have to wait," Mum said.

Aunt Maria was coming along the concrete toward

us in her dead fox and her tall hat in her wheelchair pushed by Elaine. All the other Mrs. Urs—or nine of them, anyway—were behind her, and there were quite a lot of other women, too.

"I think this is it," said Chris.

Fifteen

The two lots of us stopped, facing one another. Antony Green took the green box out of his pocket and drummed his fingers on it. Everyone's eyes went to it. It seemed twice as bright as anything in the gray seaside air. Most of the Mrs. Urs looked away rather quickly. Aunt Maria covered her face with one glove.

"Elaine," she said in her low, grieving voice, "they've got my little Naomi. How tragic!"

Elaine was staring past Aunt Maria's hat at Antony Green. When she thought she had caught his eye, she smiled. She really gave him the works. It was beyond all her other smiles, not two-line, but three-line at least. I thought she was going to split her ears. You couldn't say Antony Green took no notice, exactly. He smiled back, and of course he had a smile at least to equal Elaine's. But I saw why Aunt Maria had tried to get rid of him. His smile was perfectly friendly, but it showed he wasn't going to budge an inch.

"Good morning," he said. "I've come back to right a wrong. There have been two deaths caused by it, and a lot of unhappiness."

"What does he mean, Elaine?" Aunt Maria asked. This time it was her hurt voice. "Everyone's quite happy, aren't we, dear? And I've never killed so much as a fly in my life!"

"No, you use other people, like pincers, to kill them for you!" Chris shouted.

"Hush, dear," Aunt Maria called. "Grown-ups are talking." If she was surprised to see Chris as himself, she never showed it. She really had a nerve. Mum thought so, too. I could hear her muttering things like, "What nerve! I hope he grinds her to pulp!" until Antony Green said, "Is that all you want to say? Really?" He said it quite quietly, but it overrode all the mutterings from everyone.

"Only that I'm *surprised*," Aunt Maria said, "at someone of your education getting led into something like this. I thought you too old to make an exhibition of yourself on the seafront."

Ow! I thought. It must have been a signal. I think all the Mrs. Urs set to work then. Pitying disapproval rolled out from them in waves. Mum went bright red instantly. They followed this up with such remorse, guilt, shame, embarrassment—the feeling you have when it's your voice that rings out saying a dirty word—that everyone was writhing in seconds. One of the orphans near me quietly burst into tears.

Elaine said, "Larry, what *are* you doing?" and Larry looked as if he wanted to crawl into the sea.

Aunt Maria called gently, "Naomi, come over here, dear, away from all those people."

"No!" I said. I was still feeling the way I did at the orphanage. I knew the guilt was just another plastic bag. "You're wicked," I said.

There was a shocked gasp, and it came from Mum and some of the orphans as well as from the Mrs. Urs.

Antony Green sighed and opened the green box. "If that's the way you want it," he said. I think everybody looked at him. He stood out so, with his odd face and his strange green coat. I remember looking up at his sideface as the stuff from the box swirled around him, and I thought the one bright eye I could see looked more like a hawk's than a parrot's. The guilt still surged out from the Mrs. Urs, and I think we were all ashamed to look at that strong, invisible stuff winding up and round, into the sky, wrapping itself into the fog, collecting more strength from the smooth, dark sea. But we did look. And we saw it all pile back at Aunt Maria and the Mrs. Urs.

It was gray then, and thick and heavy and full of visions. There were hundreds of them, separate ones for each lady. I saw a great gray wolf crawl through the air toward Aunt Maria. It was slavering and snarling at first, but it suddenly jerked, leaped into the air, and fell on its side, dead. Then another wolf took its place, a smaller, brindled one, crouching miserably in the rain and obviously starving. I saw Elaine backing away from a gray, swirling image of Larry. The image was hurt, astonished, and nearly in tears. Elaine looked really upset.

Chris pushed up to Antony Green. "Elaine let me go when they were hunting me," he said.

"I know," Antony Green answered. The image of Larry got even more upset, if anything. Antony Green was staring gravely. Antony Green must have been talking to other people besides Chris and Mum, or maybe he saw some of the things while he was projecting himself from the mound. There were so many of them. People unhappy, desperate, guilty, bewildered, dozens for each lady. There were orphans crying. I saw Dad grayly several times, standing swaying up to his knees in sea, looking at death's door. I think he really did go over the cliff in some way. I even saw myself, rather to my surprise. I suppose Antony Green was trying to show me being got at by Aunt Maria, but he had done me like that picture in the book that Hester Bailey gave me, as a girl being pushed and pulled underground by horrible shadows.

I knew what he was trying to do. He was trying to force the truth of what they had done on them. But I don't think it worked, any more than when he had tried to force Naomi to be trustworthy. Some of the Mrs. Urs were as upset as Elaine. But most of them just stood there letting the visions roll around them and trying to make *us* feel guilty instead. Benita Wallins sat with her legs dangling over the edge of the promenade, crying and yelling. But I think that was really a defense. And Aunt Maria sat turned sideways in her wheelchair, looking sad and stern and teddy-bearish.

Antony Green made a last effort with her. Images poured about her. Chris, me, the orphans, Dad, a terrified gray old lady dwindling into a terrified gray cat, hundreds of things, even a crushed, suffocating image of Antony Green himself. And as a final aftermath, there was the great gray, slavering wolf again, only this time when it was shot it dissolved into a lady with her black hair spread around her and became an almost solid image of Naomi as Antony Green must have known her.

Aunt Maria just went on looking sternly out to sea. "No," she said, as the image of Naomi dissolved away, too. "Upon reflection, I have nothing in my life to reproach myself with, young man."

I think the images upset Antony Green far more than the people they were aimed at. He was pale and scarecrowlike. "Very well," he said quietly, and shut the green box with a snap. The Mrs. Urs gasped.

Aunt Maria froze into place. Then suddenly she did

not seem to be there anymore. Antony Green turned round to me and held out the green box with something balanced on top of it.

"Will you hold this steady a second while I take my coat off?" he said.

I took it carefully. Everyone, including me, made a long groaning "O—Oh" as we realized what was balanced on top of the box. It was a little tiny old lady in a fox fur and a tall hat, sitting in a little tiny wheelchair. She didn't move. I couldn't resist prodding at her with one finger, and she was hard, like a toy, but freezing cold.

Antony Green slung his green coat over his shoulder, hooked by one finger, and held out the other hand for the box. As I passed it carefully back, Mr. Phelps arrived. He was pushing Miss Phelps, who was all tiny and hunched up, in another wheelchair. This one must have come out of the ark, I think. It was made of basketwork and it had peculiar wheels. Mr. Phelps was trying to pretend he had nothing to do with it and was not really pushing it.

"Populace all gathered in the square as directed," he said in his most soldierly manner. Then he and Miss Phelps saw Aunt Maria balanced in miniature on top of the green box. They both stared. Mr. Phelps's throat slid up and down. "I didn't know that was possible," he said.

Miss Phelps said, "I wish you'd thought to give me back my wheelchair first."

"Oh, was it yours? I'm sorry," Antony Green said. He gave his longest smile. "Let's go to the square now," he said.

We went there, us and the Mrs. Urs, in a crowded, muddled procession. Antony Green walked at the head of it, smiling slightly, with his coat hung on his shoulder and the green box balanced very carefully so that the little wheels of the wheelchair did not roll the miniature Aunt Maria off the edge of the box.

The whole of Cranbury was in the square. People were sitting on the roofs of cars and crowded into the middle space, standing on benches, and rammed into doorways. I hadn't realized so many people lived in the place. None of the men had gone to work that day. I could see zombies in suits everywhere, in among women I had never seen before. Quite a lot of these pointed and made surprised noises when they saw the orphans pushing through the square behind Antony Green. I saw the clothes shop lady, the booted porter, Dr. Bailey, and Mr. Taylor the druggist, while Antony Green was pushing his way through to the war memorial in the middle, carefully holding the green box up high. Mr. Phelps and Larry followed him, shepherding the orphans. And Elaine, who obviously just has to have someone to look after, trundled Miss Phelps through in her extraordinary wheelchair and made sure she had a good place near the steps of the memorial.

Chris and I got left at the edge of the square, though, because Dad was there, too. Mum spotted him in a doorway in the distance and set off diving and fighting through the crowd to get to him. I saw her get there. But all my secret hopes of a happy ending went when I saw how horribly embarrassed Dad was to see her. He almost went backward in through the door he was leaning on to get away. He recovered a bit when Mum started speaking to him. But then Zenobia Bailey pushed up from the other side and grabbed his arm possessively. Mum spoke to her as well as Dad. Then she came pushing back to us, looking surprisingly pink and happy.

"Well," she said, "I don't know *what* went on, except that he does seem to have had some kind of accident. He says he remembers crawling out of the sea now. I suppose he lost his memory. But he's agreed to sign all the lawful documents, so that's all right."

No, it's not, I thought. But Antony Green had started to speak then, from the steps of the memorial. He speaks rather quietly, so everyone had to stop making noises to hear.

"Thank you all for coming," he said. He dropped the coat on the memorial steps so that he could hold Aunt Maria steady on the green box with both hands. "That's better," he said. "I have three things to say to you. First, the question of what to do with this lady." He held the green box up with Aunt Maria on it. "The last of the Queens," he said.

There were roars and yells all over the square: "Lock her up! Bury her! Kill her!" and some voices shouting, "No, no. She's such a character. Let her go!" Beside me, Chris was screaming, "Jump on her! Let me jump on her! I'll do it!" and Mum, in typical saintly fashion, shouted, "Don't be too hard on her, Antony!"

Antony Green looked round until everyone was quiet again. "Most of you seem to favor punishment," he said. "But you realize it won't *be* punishment, do you?" Everyone was puzzled at this. The way we all looked made Antony Green grin. "As far as this lady herself is concerned," he explained, "she was in the right all along—all her life. Nothing is going to make her see she was wrong. And the only point of punishment is to make someone see the error of their ways. If they don't see it, then what you are doing to them is vengeance, not punishment. Right? I daresay a lot of you do want vengeance. But if you do take revenge, that makes you as bad as this Mrs. Laker herself. I want to stop the wrong in Cranbury. So I am not going to take revenge. I'm simply going to put her away quietly. She probably won't even realize I have. Is that understood?"

There were grudging murmurs, and finally everyone growled that it was up to him. Antony Green grinned around at them and shoved the green box into one trouser pocket. While he was ramming Aunt Maria into his other pocket, he looked round absentmindedly. I think he had forgotten what he wanted to say. Mum says his time underground has made him forgetful, but Chris thinks he was always that way.

"Oh, yes," he said. "Here's what comes next." He pointed his thumb at the orphans. "Some of these children must belong to some of you. Who claims them?"

All the people who had pointed excitedly at the orphans earlier shouted, "Us! We do!" and came thrusting their way up to the orphans. Two-thirds of them were snatched away and hugged and hung on to. They looked pretty bewildered about it. The orphans who were left looked sad, until Mr. Phelps and Larry climbed up the steps beside Antony Green. They began holding a kind of auction. "This pretty little girl!" Mr. Phelps barked. "Any offers? How about this interesting little boy? Take that sling off your arm, boy. You're not injured. Now this fine upstanding girl."

A surprising number of people offered. As fast as one orphan was taken off, beaming and bewildered, Larry fetched another up the steps. If more than one set of people offered for the same orphan, they turned to Antony Green to settle it. He looked at each of the offers, in a humorous sort of way, with one upside-down V-eyebrow raised, and pointed a vague thumb. He seemed to be concentrating more on how hot he was. He kept flapping at his shirt, and I could see his face was shiny with sweat. It wasn't that hot, but all the people made it hotter, and by now a silvery sort of sunlight was breaking through the fog. But I think he chose the adopting parents right, for all that. He let Mr. Taylor and his Mrs. Ur, Adele, have the boy with the sling. That seemed to fit, somehow. And he gave several to just one man or one woman, over the heads of married couples. And you could see it might work, in spite of that. And he didn't let Benita Wallins have a single orphan, though she kept offering.

Then the last was a little black girl with her hair in about two hundred plaits. Larry said, "No need to put her up, Nat, that's the one I want." That was surprising. For one thing, all the orphans were so alike, you had to look at this one hard to notice she was black. For another, Larry was obviously defying Elaine.

Elaine sprang forward from beside Miss Phelps's wheelchair. "Larry! That's absolutely out of the question. I hate children."

"But I love them," said Larry. "Oh, come on, Elaine. Give it a try."

Elaine hovered and spluttered and almost refused outright, until she suddenly glanced up at Antony Green sweating on the steps above. "Oh, all *right*," she said, and even smiled. Although it was only a one-line smile, Larry let out a yell and hugged the little girl. She looked the most bewildered of the lot.

"Is that all, Antony?" asked Mr. Phelps.

"No," said Antony Green. "There is the third thing." And when all the orphan-hugging had died down, he said, "I'm giving up the green coat and leaving you today."

Everyone groaned. Somebody yelled out, sounding horrified, "Not going back into the earth?"

"Oh, no," Antony Green said, with a real shudder. "After twenty years underground like a turnip, I'm more likely to go on the road and sleep out-of-doors. And you'll agree I've got to catch up with the world. But the really important reason is this." He stood up and pulled the glistening, shining green box from his pocket again. We could tell it really *was* important, what he wanted to say. "I never wanted to take the box," he said. "I know I was right. It divides people a certain way. Maybe it didn't once, but nowadays the ones who don't have it seem to think they're not proper people without it, and then they have to go to hideous lengths to prove they *are*. So . . . " He seemed to lose the thread then and stood staring down at the meaningful shining shapes on the box, while we all waited. "So," he said, "I'm going to give back what's left of it to all of you."

He opened the box wide, until it was flat across both his hands. The stuff in it rolled out over the square in a huge trembling whirl. A lot of people crouched down to get away from it. But I think it rolled through and over anyone, whatever they did. I felt it roll through me, and I saw Mum surrounded in a tight coil of it, looking very surprised. The shimmering round Chris gave him wolf's ears for a moment. Everyone round us was gasping from it—it does fizz—and I noticed the orphan who got the birdlike bit of it had another and was holding it in his open hands, laughing the way he did before.

In the midst of it, Antony Green went down the steps and quietly walked away.

We only caught up with him because Chris happened to notice him going down the road to the seafront with one of the boatmen. Mum said, "Chris, he wants to be with his friend!" but Chris took no notice and pelted after him.

Antony Green didn't seem to mind our coming out in the boat with him. It was the first time since we had been in Cranbury that we had had anything to do with the sea, really, and it was lovely. The sea was salty swellings with silver sparkles and so gentle that even Mum couldn't be seasick, though she tried. She went pale and said it was the smell of the engine chugging away in the middle of the boat.

But Antony Green did obviously want to talk to the boatman. He was called George and he was a friend from former days. The two of them did a lot of laughing and gossiping up at the steering end of the boat, while Antony Green's hair mysteriously blew out into a mane again. George sternly kept his hair under a weathered cap and rolled cigarettes for them both and steered with his elbow and grinned.

So I asked Chris about how Elaine had let him through the line of beaters when he was a wolf. I thought it was just luck, but it wasn't quite.

Chris said, "I'm not a fool, you know. You think wolf-way, but you can still think." He had tried to go inland to get away, early that morning, but someone in a farm had shot at him and he had bolted back into the woods before he was aware. Then he was even more scared to find people assembled in the fields up at the top. "I was only in the edge of the woods," he said. "I crawled along, keeping an eye on where you were all spreading out to. I was looking for you, actually, Mig, because I knew if I hid in your path you'd pretend I wasn't there or something. But when you formed up, there was a Mrs. Ur on one side and a gunman behind you. So I crawled on till I found Elaine and took a risk on her. I lay downhill beside a log and hoped. And she stepped over the log and said, 'Keep there. Nat Phelps is hunting Germans again. Don't go uphill till he's gone past.' Then she patted my head and said, 'Good luck!' and went on downhill. I waited until Mr. Phelps had gone charging past shouting, and crawled up to the meadow again and hid in a bush there." I suppose Elaine is not so bad, really—if you are a boy.

Then Mum told us a bit about how she and Antony Green had gone round and round the woods, calling Chris. "I know every tree by now," she said. "I think I would have run about screaming, but luckily Antony needed someone sane to talk to. So I hung on in and just got more and more tired. So Antony said I could sleep in the barn while he tried a stepped-up sending for Chris. I think that's what fetched you in the end, Chris."

"Maybe," said Chris.

By then we had got right far out beyond the bay. We could see Cranbury at the edge of the sea, like a white toy village, in half-circles of little houses.

"This will do, George," Antony Green said.

George stopped the boat's engine and we drifted. Then Antony Green fetched the empty green box out of his pocket and floated it on the gentle rising, slapping waves, all opened out into two green squares with sides. He took the tiny figure of Aunt Maria in her wheelchair out of his pocket and balanced her on one half of the box. Then he gave the lot a push to send it gently floating away.

"Good riddance," said George, starting his motor again. We curved round back to Cranbury.

"Does she know? At all?" Mum asked, looking after the small floating box.

Antony Green nodded and spread his wide mouth wryly. "She thinks she's in Cranbury, going on just as usual."

"But surely . . . ," I said. "Couldn't Cranbury start up again—sort of in her mind? So we'd all be figments of her imagination there and have to do what she wanted?"

Mum looked defeated at this. It was as bad as time travel to her. Antony Green nodded again. "I have to take that risk," he said.

"And what *was* the stuff in the green box?" I said.

"You know," he said. "It's not easy to describe." But I didn't know, so he said, "Well . . . everyone has some, anyway. It was that which made Chris understand my sending or your mother understand I was buried alive."

"Oh," I said. And I broke down and howled. Everyone stared at me, except George, who turned away looking Mr. Phelpsish. "I'm not a genius!" I yowled. "I thought I was—I *know* it was the stuff of genius in the box, and I haven't got it, or I would have understood your ghost, too! It's the power of the *mind,* isn't it?"

Chris made derisive groans. It's all right for him. He's sure he *is* a genius.

Mum said, "Mig, do stop being silly!"

"She's not being silly," Antony Green said. "*You* didn't see my projection's mouth move?" he asked me. I shook my head and snorted sobs in all directions. "And you expect to see a mouth move when someone talks," he said. "Sometimes what is really there gets covered up by what you *expect* to see. That's all." And he stopped my effort to cry louder than ever by saying, "So now you know, you won't very often be deceived by your expectations. People who understand instantly might be deceived a second time, but not you."

George changed the subject then by saying, "Got much of the stuff left yourself, Tony? Always seemed to me you didn't need a green box."

"Let's see." Antony Green ran his hands thoughtfully along the sides of the boat. Where his hands had been, the white plastic-sort-of boat broke out in multicolored glitters. It seemed to have colored glass stuck into it. He looked at it carefully. "Diamonds, mostly," he said. "Emeralds, rubies, sapphires, and so on." He looked at George's face. "I kid you not. It's been building inside me for twenty years, George."

"Take it off, darn you!" George shouted. "What do I do with a bloody tiara for a boat? Pardon my language," he added to Mum.

Antony Green scooped his hands along the edges of the boat and rattled the glittering stones in two handfuls down into the green moldy bottom of the boat. "That better?"

George bent his hatted head and stared, grudgingly. "Think you could make it pearls, instead?" he said. "More natural and easier to sell, those are."

So Antony Green ran the handfuls of jewels through his hands again, and they rattled down like peas, only pinkish and whitish and nacreous. (Now there's a good word! Only a genius would have used *nacreous*.) We left George sorting them out into sizes after we landed and walked back along the seafront to Aunt Maria's house. Antony Green, a bit to my surprise, came with us, and we met the Phelpses on the way. Miss Phelps was very cheery, but Mr. Phelps was long-suffering. "Pity you can't stay," he said stiffly.

We all came up the street together. And it was lucky that Aunt Maria's house didn't have a garage at one side the way the Phelpses did across the road. Aunt Maria's house was not there anymore. There was no gap. Elaine's house was up against the house on the other side of Aunt Maria's. Mum's rattletrap little car was parked in the street between the two.

"Oh, dear!" said Mum, thinking of all our clothes that seemed to have gone for good.

"I rescued one or two important things," said Miss Phelps.

She had, sort of. Mum's pea green knitting was on the bonnet of the car with Chris's guitar and his sacred work-books. My precious locked book slithered off the bonnet and fell in the road as a desperate gray cat jumped off the knitting and ran toward us, mewing for help and comfort.

"Lavinia!" cried Mum. "I'd clean forgotten about her."

Lavinia instantly lay soppily on her back on the pavement, waving paws in the air. Antony Green said, in a tired way, "I'd better see to her, too." He squatted down and put his hand on Lavinia's squirming chest. She most ungratefully dug all her front claws into him and treadled his hand with her back ones. She squalled and tried to bite him. Antony Green's hand was in a worse state than Mr. Phelps's cheek by the time he had forced the gray cat to spread into woman shape. He had to keep forcing, too. Every time he relaxed, Lavinia shrank back into a gray fluffy cat. At last, he forced her head at least to appear as a flatfaced old woman's head with wild gray hair. "Don't you want to be turned back?" he asked the face.

"No," said Lavinia. "Let me be a cat. Please. So much more restful."

He looked up at us. Mum said, "I bet Auntie led her a dreadful dance."

Chris said, "Running in the night was fun."

"I *loved* being a cat," I said. "Let her, if she wants."

So Antony Green took his hand away, and Lavinia shrank gladly into a cat again.

"She had next to no brain, poor woman," Miss Phelps said, when I kissed her good-bye for rescuing my book. Miss Phelps had saved all the right things, whatever Mum says.

Mum, naturally, took Lavinia back to London with us in the car. Now she runs adoringly after Mum whenever Mum is in. Chris and I treat Lavinia with the contempt a floppy-cushion cat deserves, but I suppose she cheers Mum up during the times Antony Green disappears.

Antony Green begged a lift with us to London. Then he went away. He said he couldn't bear to be under a roof for a while.

He has other troubles. He turns up every so often, sometimes exhausted and shabby, sometimes ordinary, and once looking very smart, saying he had just flown from New York on the Concorde. And he talks and talks to all of us. One of his troubles is that poor Zoe Green killed herself that morning they plowed up the mound. Antony is sort of resigned, because he thought he had been underground for about a hundred years and had got used to the idea of never seeing his mother again. But he keeps wondering, the way things worked in Cranbury, whether she didn't give her life instead of him.

I tell him it is just a stupid waste. If only we'd met her earlier, or later—when we were time traveling, anyway—we could have shown her he was alive. And I can't think how she missed seeing him when he was capering round the town. But I am glad Mum didn't go dotty that way when Chris and I were missing.

Antony Green has trouble adjusting to losing twenty years, too. He says things have leaped onward, and he goes to all sorts of classes and lectures to catch up. When he comes to see us, he sits leaning over our TV as if it was a teaching machine. But his worst trouble is dreaming about being buried. We all know how that feels. Mum says she doubts Antony will ever be quite normal again.

I sometimes wonder if Chris will be, either. He seems quite usual. But sometimes he gets a wistful wolf look in his eyes and talks about how marvelous it is to run in the night. "Yes, but think of when it rained," I say. And Chris says yes, he knows, but he has decided not to be a genius at math anymore. He's going to make films of wildlife. Mum had to buy him a movie camera for his birthday and she says it nearly broke her.

P.S. That was all six months ago now. I have spent the time rewriting this biography and doing to the end. Sometimes I have added bits and sometimes I have cheated a bit so that it looks as if I wrote more than I did. Chris says if I really wrote that screed at Aunt Maria's, I wouldn't have had time to do anything else. But I want it to be good when I finish it. And I want to finish it soon because when Antony Green comes to see us, when he's in a good mood and we all go out together, things always happen. I want to put those in a book, too.

The divorce came through. Dad rang up yesterday to say he had married Zenobia Bailey. The silly fool.

Antony Green has just turned up again. Mum and he came in while I was writing my P.S. and made their Special Announcement. Chris looked up from his stack of animal photographs, and we both made faces. I said we must be the only people in the world whose mother is going to marry an ex-ghost.

Chris says that's another thing to blame Aunt Maria for. But I don't think he meant it.